SAY CHEESE AND DIE!

Look for other **Goosebumps** books
by R.L. Stine:

Goosebumps®

SAY CHEESE AND DIE!

R.L. STINE

SCHOLASTIC INC.
New York Toronto London Auckland Sydney
Mexico City New Delhi Hong Kong Buenos Aires

ISBN 0-439-56842-0

12 11 10   6 7 8/0

Printed in the U.S.A.   40

First Scholastic printing, November 1992

"There's nothing to do in Pitts Landing," Michael Warner said, his hands shoved into the pockets of his faded denim cutoffs.

"Yeah. Pitts Landing is the pits," Greg Banks said.

Doug Arthur and Shari Walker muttered their agreement.

Pitts Landing is the Pits. That was the town slogan, according to Greg and his three friends. Actually, Pitts Landing wasn't much different from a lot of small towns with quiet streets of shady lawns and comfortable, old houses.

But here it was, a balmy fall afternoon, and the four friends were hanging around Greg's driveway, kicking at the gravel, wondering what to do for fun and excitement.

"Let's go to Grover's and see if the new comic books have come in," Doug suggested.

"We don't have any money, Bird," Greg told him.

Everyone called Doug "Bird" because he looked

a lot like a bird. A better nickname might have been "Stork." He had long, skinny legs and took long, storklike steps. Under his thick tuft of brown hair, which he seldom brushed, he had small, birdlike brown eyes and a long nose that curved like a beak. Doug didn't really like being called Bird, but he was used to it.

"We can still *look* at the comics," Bird insisted.

"Until Grover starts yelling at you," Shari said. She puffed out her cheeks and did a pretty good imitation of the gruff store owner: *"Are you paying or staying?"*

"He thinks he's cool," Greg said, laughing at her imitation. "He's such a jerk."

"I think the new *X-Force* is coming in this week," Bird said.

"You should join the X-Force," Greg said, giving his pal a playful shove. "You could be Bird Man. You'd be great!"

"We should *all* join the X-Force," Michael said. "If we were super-heroes, maybe we'd have something to do."

"No, we wouldn't," Shari quickly replied. "There's no crime to fight in Pitts Landing."

"We could fight crabgrass," Bird suggested. He was the joker in the group.

The others laughed. The four of them had been friends for a long time. Greg and Shari lived next door to each other, and their parents were best friends. Bird and Michael lived on the next block.

"How about a baseball game?" Michael suggested. "We could go down to the playground."

"No way," Shari said. "You can't play with only four people." She pushed back a strand of her crimped, black hair that had fallen over her face. Shari was wearing an oversized yellow sweatshirt over bright green leggings.

"Maybe we'll find some other kids there," Michael said, picking up a handful of gravel from the drive and letting it sift through his chubby fingers. Michael had short red hair, blue eyes, and a face full of freckles. He wasn't exactly fat, but no one would ever call him skinny.

"Come on, let's play baseball," Bird urged. "I need the practice. My Little League starts in a couple of days."

"Little League? In the fall?" Shari asked.

"It's a new fall league. The first game is Tuesday after school," Bird explained.

"Hey — we'll come watch you," Greg said.

"We'll come watch you strike out," Shari added. Her hobby was teasing Bird.

"What position are you playing?" Greg asked.

"Backstop," Michael cracked.

No one laughed. Michael's jokes always fell flat.

Bird shrugged. "Probably the outfield. How come *you're* not playing, Greg?"

With his big shoulders and muscular arms and legs, Greg was the natural athlete of the group. He was blond and good-looking, with flashing

3

gray-green eyes and a wide, friendly smile.

"My brother Terry was supposed to go sign me up, but he forgot," Greg said, making a disgusted face.

"Where *is* Terry?" Shari asked. She had a tiny crush on Greg's older brother.

"He got a job Saturdays and after school. At the Dairy Freeze," Greg told her.

"Let's go to the Dairy Freeze!" Michael exclaimed enthusiastically.

"We don't have any money — remember?" Bird said glumly.

"Terry'll give us free cones," Michael said, turning a hopeful gaze on Greg.

"Yeah. Free cones. But no ice cream in them," Greg told him. "You know what a straight-arrow my brother is."

"This is boring," Shari complained, watching a robin hop across the sidewalk. "It's boring standing around talking about how bored we are."

"We could *sit down* and talk about how bored we are," Bird suggested, twisting his mouth into the goofy half-smile he always wore when he was making a dumb joke.

"Let's take a walk or a jog or something," Shari insisted. She made her way across the lawn and began walking, balancing her white high-tops on the edge of the curb, waving her arms like a high-wire performer.

The boys followed, imitating her in an impromptu game of Follow the Leader, all of them

4

balancing on the curb edge as they walked.

A curious cocker spaniel came bursting out of the neighbors' hedge, yapping excitedly. Shari stopped to pet him. The dog, its stub of a tail wagging furiously, licked her hand a few times. Then the dog lost interest and disappeared back into the hedge.

The four friends continued down the block, playfully trying to knock each other off the curb as they walked. They crossed the street and continued on past the school. A couple of guys were shooting baskets, and some little kids played kickball on the practice baseball diamond, but no one they knew.

The road curved away from the school. They followed it past familiar houses. Then, just beyond a small wooded area, they stopped and looked up a sloping lawn, the grass uncut for weeks, tall weeds poking out everywhere, the shrubs ragged and overgrown.

At the top of the lawn, nearly hidden in the shadows of enormous, old oak trees, sprawled a large, ramshackle house. The house, anyone could see, had once been grand. It was gray shingle, three stories tall, with a wraparound screened porch, a sloping red roof, and tall chimneys on either end. But the broken windows on the second floor, the cracked, weather-stained shingles, the bare spots on the roof, and the shutters hanging loosely beside the dust-smeared windows were evidence of the house's neglect.

Everyone in Pitts Landing knew it as the Coffman house. Coffman was the name painted on the mailbox that tilted on its broken pole over the front walk.

But the house had been deserted for years — ever since Greg and his friends could remember.

And people liked to tell weird stories about the house: ghost stories and wild tales about murders and ghastly things that happened there. Most likely, none of them were true.

"Hey — I know what we can do for excitement," Michael said, staring up at the house bathed in shadows.

"Huh? What are you talking about?" Greg asked warily.

"Let's go into the Coffman house," Michael said, starting to make his way across the weed-choked lawn.

"Whoa. Are you crazy?" Greg called, hurrying to catch up to him.

"Let's go in," Michael said, his blue eyes catching the light of the late afternoon sun filtering down through the tall oak trees. "We wanted an adventure. Something a little exciting, right? Come on — let's check it out."

Greg hesitated and stared up at the house. A cold chill ran down his back.

Before he could reply, a dark form leapt up from the shadows of the tall weeds and attacked him!

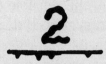

2

Greg toppled backwards onto the ground. "Aah!" he screamed. Then he realized the others were laughing.

"It's that dumb cocker spaniel!" Shari cried. "He followed us!"

"Go home, dog. Go home!" Bird shooed the dog away.

The dog trotted to the curb, turned around, and stared back at them, its stubby tail wagging furiously.

Feeling embarrassed that he'd become so frightened, Greg slowly pulled himself to his feet, expecting his friends to give him grief. But they were staring up at the Coffman house thoughtfully.

"Yeah, Michael's right," Bird said, slapping Michael hard on the back, so hard Michael winced and turned to slug Bird. "Let's see what it's like in there."

"No way," Greg said, hanging back. "I mean,

the place is kind of creepy, don't you think?"

"So?" Shari challenged him, joining Michael and Bird, who repeated her question: "So?"

"So . . . I don't know," Greg replied. He didn't like being the sensible one of the group. Everyone always made fun of the sensible one. He'd rather be the wild and crazy one. But, somehow, he always ended up sensible.

"I don't think we should go in there," he said, staring up at the neglected old house.

"Are you chicken?" Bird asked.

"Chicken!" Michael joined in.

Bird began to cluck loudly, tucking his hands into his armpits and flapping his arms. With his beady eyes and beaky nose, he looked just like a chicken.

Greg didn't want to laugh, but he couldn't help it.

Bird *always* made him laugh.

The clucking and flapping seemed to end the discussion. They were standing at the foot of the broken concrete steps that led up to the screened porch.

"Look. The window next to the front door is broken," Shari said. "We can just reach in and open the door."

"This is cool," Michael said enthusiastically.

"Are we really doing this?" Greg, being the sensible one, had to ask. "I mean — what about Spidey?"

Spidey was a weird-looking man of fifty or sixty they'd all seen lurking about town. He dressed entirely in black and crept along on long, slender legs. He looked just like a black spider, so the kids all called him Spidey.

Most likely he was a homeless guy. No one really knew anything about him — where he'd come from, where he lived. But a lot of kids had seen him hanging around the Coffman house.

"Maybe Spidey doesn't like visitors," Greg warned.

But Shari was already reaching in through the broken windowpane to unlock the front door. And after little effort, she turned the brass knob and the heavy wooden door swung open.

One by one, they stepped into the front entry-way, Greg reluctantly bringing up the rear. It was dark inside the house. Only narrow beams of sunlight managed to trickle down through the heavy trees in front, creating pale circles of light on the worn brown carpet at their feet.

The floorboards squeaked as Greg and his friends made their way past the living room, which was bare except for a couple of overturned grocery store cartons against one wall.

Spidey's furniture? Greg wondered.

The living room carpet, as threadbare as the one in the entryway, had a dark oval stain in the center of it. Greg and Bird, stopping in the doorway, both noticed it at the same time.

9

"Think it's blood?" Bird asked, his tiny eyes lighting up with excitement.

Greg felt a chill on the back of his neck. "Probably ketchup," he replied. Bird laughed and slapped him hard on the back.

Shari and Michael were exploring the kitchen. They were staring at the dust-covered kitchen counter as Greg stepped up behind them. He saw immediately what had captured their attention. Two fat, gray mice were standing on the countertop, staring back at them.

"They're cute," Shari said. "They look just like cartoon mice."

The sound of her voice made the two rodents scamper along the counter, around the sink, and out of sight.

"They're gross," Michael said, making a disgusted face. "I think they were rats — not mice."

"Rats have long tails. Mice don't," Greg told him.

"They were definitely rats," Bird muttered, pushing past them and into the hallway. He disappeared toward the front of the house.

Shari reached up and pulled open a cabinet over the counter. Empty. "I guess Spidey never uses the kitchen," she said.

"Well, I didn't *think* he was a gourmet chef," Greg joked.

He followed her into the long, narrow dining room, as bare and dusty as the other rooms. A low chandelier still hung from the ceiling, so brown with caked dust, it was impossible to tell that it was glass.

"Looks like a haunted house," Greg said softly.

"Boo," Shari replied.

"There's not much to see in here," Greg complained, following her back to the dark hallway. "Unless you get a thrill from dustballs."

Suddenly, a loud *crack* made him jump.

Shari laughed and squeezed his shoulder.

"What was *that*?" he cried, unable to stifle his fear.

"Old houses *do* things like that," she said. "They make noises for no reason at all."

"I think we should leave," Greg insisted, embarrassed again that he'd acted so frightened. "I mean, it's boring in here."

"It's kind of exciting being somewhere we're not supposed to be," Shari said, peeking into a dark, empty room — probably a den or study at one time.

"I guess," Greg replied uncertainly.

They bumped into Michael. "Where's Bird?" Greg asked.

"I think he went down in the basement," Michael replied.

"Huh? The basement?"

Michael pointed to an open door at the right of the hallway. "The stairs are there."

The three of them made their way to the top of

the stairs. They peered down into the darkness. "Bird?"

From somewhere deep in the basement, his voice floated up to them in a horrified scream: "Help! It's got me! Somebody — please help! It's *got* me!"

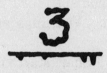

3

"It's got me! It's got me!"

At the sound of Bird's terrified cries, Greg pushed past Shari and Michael, who stood frozen in open-mouthed horror. Practically flying down the steep stairway, Greg called out to his friend. "I'm coming, Bird! What *is it*?"

His heart pounding, Greg stopped at the bottom of the stairs, every muscle tight with fear. His eyes searched frantically through the smoky light pouring in from the basement windows up near the ceiling.

"Bird?"

There he was, sitting comfortably, calmly, on an overturned metal trash can, his legs crossed, a broad smile on his birdlike face. "Gotcha," he said softly, and burst out laughing.

"What *is* it? What *happened*?" came the frightened voices of Shari and Michael. They clamored down the stairs, coming to a stop beside Greg.

It took them only a few seconds to scope out the situation.

"Another dumb joke?" Michael asked, his voice still trembling with fear.

"Bird — you were goofing on us again?" Shari asked, shaking her head.

Enjoying his moment, Bird nodded, with his peculiar half-grin. "You guys are too easy," he scoffed.

"But, Doug — " Shari started. She only called him Doug when she was upset with him. "Haven't you ever heard of the boy who cried wolf? What if something bad happens sometime, and you really need help, and we think you're just goofing?"

"What could happen?" Bird replied smugly. He stood up and gestured around the basement. "Look — it's brighter down here than upstairs."

He was right. Sunlight from the back yard cascaded down through four long windows at ground level, near the ceiling of the basement.

"I still think we should get out of here," Greg insisted, his eyes moving quickly around the large, cluttered room.

Behind Bird's overturned trash can stood an improvised table made out of a sheet of plywood resting on four paint cans. A nearly flat mattress, dirty and stained, rested against the wall, a faded wool blanket folded at the foot.

"Spidey must *live* down here!" Michael exclaimed.

Bird kicked his way through a pile of empty food boxes that had been tossed all over the floor — TV dinners, mostly. "Hey, a Hungry Man dinner!" he exclaimed. "Where does Spidey heat these up?"

"Maybe he eats them frozen," Shari suggested. "You know. Like Popsicles."

She made her way toward a towering oak wardrobe and pulled open the doors. "Wow! This is *excellent*!" she declared. "Look!" She pulled out a ratty-looking fur coat and wrapped it around her shoulders. "Excellent!" she repeated, twirling in the old coat.

From across the room, Greg could see that the wardrobe was stuffed with old clothing. Michael and Bird hurried to join Shari and began pulling out strange-looking pairs of bell-bottom pants, yellowed dress shirts with pleats down the front, tie-dyed neckties that were about a foot wide, and bright-colored scarves and bandannas.

"Hey, guys — " Greg warned. "Don't you think maybe those belong to somebody?"

Bird spun around, a fuzzy red boa wrapped around his neck and shoulders. "Yeah. These are Spidey's dress-up clothes," he cracked.

"Check out this *baad* hat," Shari said, turning around to show off the bright purple, wide-brimmed hat she had pulled on.

"Neat," Michael said, examining a long blue cape. "This stuff must be at least twenty-five years old. It's awesome. How could someone just leave it here?"

"Maybe they're coming back for it," Greg suggested.

As his friends explored the contents of the wardrobe, Greg wandered to the other end of the large basement. A furnace occupied the far wall, its ducts covered in thick cobwebs. Partially hidden by the furnace ducts, Greg could see stairs, probably leading to an outside exit.

Wooden shelves lined the adjoining wall, cluttered with old paint cans, rags, newspapers, and rusty tools.

Whoever lived here must have been a real handyman, Greg thought, examining a wooden worktable in front of the shelves. A metal vise was clamped to the edge of the worktable. Greg turned the handle, expecting the jaws of the vise to open.

But to his surprise, as he turned the vise handle, a door just above the worktable popped open. Greg pulled the door all the way open, revealing a hidden cabinet shelf.

Resting on the shelf was a camera.

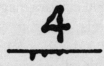

4

For a long moment, Greg just stared at the camera.

Something told him the camera was hidden away for a reason.

Something told him he shouldn't touch it. He should close the secret door and walk away.

But he couldn't resist it.

He reached onto the hidden shelf and took the camera in his hands.

It pulled out easily. Then, to Greg's surprise, the door instantly snapped shut with a loud *bang*.

Weird, he thought, turning the camera in his hands.

What a strange place to leave a camera. Why would someone put it here? If it were valuable enough to hide in a secret cabinet, why didn't they take it with them?

Greg eagerly examined the camera. It was large and surprisingly heavy, with a long lens. Perhaps a telephoto lens, he thought.

Greg was very interested in cameras. He had an inexpensive automatic camera, which took okay snapshots. But he was saving his allowance in hopes of buying a really good camera with a lot of lenses.

He loved looking at camera magazines, studying the different models, picking out the ones he wanted to buy.

Sometimes he daydreamed about traveling around the world, going to amazing places, mountaintops and hidden jungle rivers. He'd take photos of everything he saw and become a famous photographer.

His camera at home was just too crummy. That's why all his pictures came out too dark or too light, and everyone in them had glowing red dots in their eyes.

Greg wondered if this camera was any good.

Raising the viewfinder to his eye, he sighted around the room. He came to a stop on Michael, who was wearing two bright yellow feather boas and a white Stetson hat and had climbed to the top of the steps to pose.

"Wait! Hold it!" Greg cried, moving closer, raising the camera to his eye. "Let me take your picture, Michael."

"Where'd you find that?" Bird asked.

"Does that thing have film in it?" Michael demanded.

"I don't know," Greg said. "Let's see."

Leaning against the railing, Michael struck what he considered a sophisticated pose.

Greg pointed the camera up and focused carefully. It took a short while for his finger to locate the shutter button. "Okay, ready? Say cheese."

"Cheddar," Michael said, grinning down at Greg as he held his pose against the railing.

"Very funny. Michael's a riot," Bird said sarcastically.

Greg centered Michael in the viewfinder frame, then pressed the shutter button.

The camera clicked and flashed.

Then it made an electronic whirring sound. A slot pulled open on the bottom, and a cardboard square slid out.

"Hey — it's one of those automatic-developing cameras," Greg exclaimed. He pulled the square of cardboard out and examined it. "Look — the picture is starting to develop."

"Let me see," Michael called down, leaning on the railing.

But before he could start down the stairs, everyone heard a loud crunching sound.

They all looked up to the source of the sound — and saw the railing break away and Michael go sailing over the edge.

"Noooooo!" Michael screamed as he toppled to the floor, arms outstretched, the feather boas flying behind him like animal tails.

He turned in the air, then hit the concrete hard

on his back, his eyes frozen wide in astonishment and fright.

He bounced once.

Then cried out again: "My ankle! Owwww! My ankle!" He grabbed at the injured ankle, then quickly let go with a loud gasp. It hurt too much to touch it.

"*Ohhh* — my ankle!"

Still holding the camera and the photo, Greg rushed to Michael. Shari and Bird did the same.

"We'll go get help," Shari told Michael, who was still on his back, groaning in pain.

But then they heard the ceiling creak.

Footsteps. Above them.

Someone was in the house.

Someone was approaching the basement stairs.

They were going to be caught.

5

The footsteps overhead grew louder.

The four friends exchanged frightened glances. "We've got to get *out* of here," Shari whispered.

The ceiling creaked.

"You can't leave me here!" Michael protested. He pulled himself to a sitting position.

"Quick — stand up," Bird instructed.

Michael struggled to his feet. "I can't stand on this foot." His face revealed his panic.

"We'll help you," Shari said, turning her eyes to Bird. "I'll take one arm. You take the other."

Bird obediently moved forward and pulled Michael's arm around his shoulder.

"Okay, let's move!" Shari whispered, supporting Michael from the other side.

"But how do we get out?" Bird asked breathlessly.

The footsteps grew louder. The ceiling creaked under their weight.

"We can't go up the stairs," Michael whispered, leaning on Shari and Bird.

"There's another stairway behind the furnace," Greg told them, pointing.

"It leads out?" Michael asked, wincing from his ankle pain.

"Probably."

Greg led the way. "Just pray the door isn't padlocked or something."

"We're praying. We're praying!" Bird declared.

"We're outta here!" Shari said, groaning under the weight of Michael's arm.

Leaning heavily against Shari and Bird, Michael hobbled after Greg, and they made their way to the stairs behind the furnace. The stairs, they saw, led to wooden double doors up on ground level.

"I don't see a padlock," Greg said warily. "Please, doors — be open!"

"Hey — who's down there?" an angry man's voice called from behind them.

"It's — it's Spidey!" Michael stammered.

"Hurry!" Shari urged, giving Greg a frightened push. "Come *on!*"

Greg set the camera down on the top step. Then he reached up and grabbed the handles of the double doors.

"Who's down there?"

Spidey sounded closer, angrier.

"The doors could be locked from the outside,"
Greg whispered, hesitating.

"Just *push* them, man!" Bird pleaded.

Greg took a deep breath and pushed with all his
strength.

The doors didn't budge.

"We're trapped," he told them.

6

"Now what?" Michael whined.

"Try again," Bird urged Greg. "Maybe they're just stuck." He slid out from under Michael's arm. "Here. I'll help you."

Greg moved over to give Bird room to step up beside him. "Ready?" he asked. "One, two, three — *push!*"

Both boys pushed against the heavy wooden doors with all their might.

And the doors swung open.

"Okay! *Now* we're outta here!" Shari declared happily.

Picking up the camera, Greg led the way out. The back yard, he saw, was as weed-choked and overgrown as the front. An enormous limb had fallen off an old oak tree, probably during a storm, and was lying half in the tree, half on the ground.

Somehow, Bird and Shari managed to drag Michael up the steps and onto the grass. "Can you walk? Try it," Bird said.

Still leaning against the two of them, Michael reluctantly pushed his foot down on the ground. He lifted it. Then pushed it again. "Hey, it feels a little better," he said, surprised.

"Then let's go," Bird said.

They ran to the overgrown hedge that edged along the side of the yard, Michael on his own now, stepping gingerly on the bad ankle, doing his best to keep up. Then, staying in the shadow of the hedge, they made their way around the house to the front.

"All *right*!" Bird cried happily as they reached the street. "We made it!"

Gasping for breath, Greg stopped at the curb and turned back toward the house. "Look!" he cried, pointing up to the living room window.

A dark figure stood in the window, hands pressed against the glass.

"It's Spidey," Shari said.

"He's just — staring at us," Michael cried.

"Weird," Greg said. "Let's go."

They didn't stop till they got to Michael's house, a sprawling redwood ranch-style house behind a shady front lawn.

"How's the ankle?" Greg asked.

"It's loosened up a lot. It doesn't even hurt that much," Michael said.

"Man, you could've been *killed*!" Bird declared, wiping sweat off his forehead with the sleeve of his T-shirt.

"Thanks for reminding me," Michael said dryly.

"Lucky thing you've got all that extra padding," Bird teased.

"Shut up," Michael muttered.

"Well, you guys wanted adventure," Shari said, leaning back against the trunk of a tree.

"That guy Spidey is definitely weird," Bird said, shaking his head.

"You see the way he was staring at us?" Michael asked. "All dressed in black and everything? He looked like some kind of zombie or something."

"He saw us," Greg said softly, suddenly feeling a chill of dread. "He saw us very clearly. We'd better stay away from there."

"What for?" Michael demanded. "It isn't his house. He's just sleeping there. We could call the police on him."

"But if he's really crazy or something, there's no telling what he might do," Greg replied thoughtfully.

"Aw, he's not going to do anything," Shari said quietly. "Spidey doesn't want trouble. He just wants to be left alone."

"Yeah," Michael agreed quickly. "He didn't want us messing with his stuff. That's why he yelled like that and came after us."

Michael was leaning over, rubbing his ankle.

"Hey, where's my picture?" he demanded, straightening up and turning to Greg.

"Huh?"

"You know. The picture you snapped. With the camera."

"Oh. Right." Greg suddenly realized he still had the camera gripped tightly in his hand. He set it down carefully on the grass and reached into his back pocket. "I put it in here when we started to run," he explained.

"Well? Did it come out?" Michael demanded.

The three of them huddled around Greg to get a view of the snapshot.

"Whoa — hold on a minute!" Greg cried, staring hard at the small, square photo. "Something's wrong. What's going *on* here?"

7

The four friends gaped at the photograph in Greg's hand, their mouths dropping open in surprise.

The camera had caught Michael in midair as he fell through the broken railing to the floor.

"That's impossible!" Shari cried.

"You snapped the picture *before* I fell!" Michael declared, grabbing the photo out of Greg's hand so that he could study it close up. "I remember it."

"You remembered wrong," Bird said, moving to get another look at it over Michael's shoulder. "You were falling, man. What a great action shot." He picked up the camera. "This is a good camera you stole, Greg."

"I didn't steal it" — Greg started — "I mean, I didn't realize — "

"I wasn't falling!" Michael insisted, tilting the picture in his hand, studying it from every angle. "I was posing, remember? I had a big, goofy smile on my face, and I was posing."

28

"I remember the goofy smile," Bird said, handing the camera back to Greg. "Do you have any *other* expression?"

"You're not funny, Bird," Michael muttered. He pocketed the picture.

"Weird," Greg said. He glanced at his watch. "Hey — I've got to get going."

He said good-bye to the others and headed for home. The afternoon sun was lowering behind a cluster of palm trees, casting long, shifting shadows over the sidewalk.

He had promised his mother he'd straighten up his room and help with the vacuuming before dinner. And now he was late.

What was that strange car in the drive? he wondered, jogging across the neighbor's lawn toward his house.

It was a navy-blue Taurus station wagon. Brand new.

Dad picked up our new car! he realized.

Wow! Greg stopped to admire it. It still had the sticker glued to the door window. He pulled open the driver's door, leaned in, and smelled the vinyl upholstery.

Mmmmmm. That new-car smell.

He inhaled deeply again. It smelled so good. So fresh and new.

He closed the door hard, appreciating the solid *clunk* it made as it closed.

What a great new car, he thought excitedly.

He raised the camera to his eye and took a few steps back off the drive.

I've *got* to take a picture of this, he thought. To remember what the car was like when it was totally new.

He backed up until he had framed the entire profile of the station wagon in the viewfinder. Then he pressed the shutter button.

As before, the camera clicked loudly, the flash flashed, and with an electronic *whirr*, a square undeveloped photo of gray and yellow slid out of the bottom.

Carrying the camera and the snapshot, Greg ran into the house through the front door. "I'm home!" he called. "Down in a minute!" And hurried up the carpeted stairs to his room.

"Greg? Is that you? Your father is home," his mother called from downstairs.

"I know. Be right down. Sorry I'm late!" Greg shouted back.

I'd better hide the camera, he decided. If Mom or Dad see it, they'll want to know whose it is and where I got it. And I won't be able to answer those questions.

"Greg — did you see the new car? Are you coming down?" his mother called impatiently from the foot of the stairs.

"I'm coming!" he yelled.

His eyes searched frantically for a good hiding place.

Under his bed?

No. His mom might vacuum under there and discover it.

Then Greg remembered the secret compartment in his headboard. He had discovered the compartment years ago when his parents had bought him a new bedroom set. Quickly, he shoved the camera in.

Peering into the mirror above his dresser, he gave his blond hair a quick brush, rubbed a black soot smudge off his cheek with one hand, then started for the door.

He stopped at the doorway.

The snapshot of the car. Where had he put it?

It took a few seconds to remember that he had tossed it onto his bed. Curious about how it came out, he turned back to retrieve it.

"Oh, no!"

He uttered a low cry as he gazed at the snapshot.

8

What's going on here? Greg wondered.

He brought the photo up close to his face.

This isn't right, he thought. How can this *be*?

The blue Taurus station wagon in the photo was a mess. It looked as if it had been in a terrible accident. The windshield was shattered. Metal was twisted and bent. The door on the driver's side was caved in.

The car appeared *totaled*!

"This is impossible!" Greg uttered aloud.

"Greg, where *are* you?" his mother called. "We're all hungry, and you're keeping us waiting."

"Sorry," he answered, unable to take his eyes off the snapshot. "Coming."

He shoved the photo into his top dresser drawer and made his way downstairs. The image of the totaled car burned in his mind.

Just to make sure, he crossed the living room

and peeked out of the front window to the driveway.

There stood the station wagon, sparkling in the glow of the setting sun. Shiny and perfect.

He turned and walked into the dining room where his brother and his parents were already seated. "The new wagon is awesome, Dad," Greg said, trying to shake the snapshot's image from his thoughts.

But he kept seeing the twisted metal, the caved-in driver's door, the shattered windshield.

"After dinner," Greg's dad announced happily, "I'm taking you all for a drive in the new car!"

9

"Mmmm. This is great chicken, Mom," Greg's brother Terry said, chewing as he talked.

"Thanks for the compliment," Mrs. Banks said dryly, "but it's veal — not chicken."

Greg and his dad burst out laughing. Terry's face grew bright red. "Well," he said, still chewing, "it's such excellent veal, it tastes as good as chicken!"

"I don't know why I bother to cook," Mrs. Banks sighed.

Mr. Banks changed the subject. "How are things at the Dairy Freeze?" he asked.

"We ran out of vanilla this afternoon," Terry said, forking a small potato and shoving it whole into his mouth. He chewed it briefly, then gulped it down. "People were annoyed about that."

"I don't think I can go for the ride," Greg said, staring down at his dinner, which he'd hardly touched. "I mean — "

"Why not?" his father asked.

"Well . . ." Greg searched his mind for a good reason. He needed to make one up, but his mind was a blank.

He couldn't tell them the truth.

That he had taken a snapshot of Michael, and it showed Michael falling. Then a few seconds later, Michael had fallen.

And now he had taken a picture of the new car. And the car was wrecked in the photo.

Greg didn't really know what it meant. But he was suddenly filled with this powerful feeling, of dread, of fear, of . . . he didn't know what.

A kind of troubled feeling he'd never had before.

But he couldn't tell them any of that. It was too weird. Too *crazy*.

"I . . . made plans to go over to Michael's," he lied, staring down at his plate.

"Well, call him and tell him you'll see him tomorrow," Mr. Banks said, slicing his veal. "That's no problem."

"Well, I'm kind of not feeling very well, either," Greg said.

"What's wrong?" Mrs. Banks asked with instant concern. "Do you have a temperature? I thought you looked a little flushed when you came in."

"No," Greg replied uncomfortably. "No temperature. I just feel kind of tired, not very hungry."

"Can I have your chicken — I mean, veal?" Terry asked eagerly. He reached his fork across

35

the table and nabbed the cutlet off Greg's plate.

"Well, a nice ride might make you feel better," Greg's dad said, eyeing Greg suspiciously. "You know, some fresh air. You can stretch out in the back if you want."

"But, Dad — " Greg stopped. He had used up all the excuses he could think of. They would *never* believe him if he said he needed to stay home and do homework on a Saturday night!

"You're coming with us, and that's final," Mr. Banks said, still studying Greg closely. "You've been dying for this new wagon to arrive. I really don't understand your problem."

Neither do I, Greg admitted to himself.

I don't understand it at all. Why am I so afraid of riding in the new car? Just because there's something wrong with that stupid camera?

I'm being silly, Greg thought, trying to shake away the feeling of dread that had taken away his appetite.

"Okay, Dad, Great," he said, forcing a smile. "I'll come."

"Are there any more potatoes?" Terry asked.

10

"It's so easy to drive," Mr. Banks said, accelerating onto the entry ramp to the freeway. "It handles like a small car, not like a station wagon."

"Plenty of room back here, Dad," Terry said, scooting low in the back seat beside Greg, raising his knees to the back of the front seat.

"Hey, look — there's a drink holder that pulls out from the dash!" Greg's mother exclaimed. "That's neat."

"Awesome, Mom," Terry said sarcastically.

"Well, we never had a drink holder before," Mrs. Banks replied. She turned back to the two boys. "Are your seat belts buckled? Do they work properly?"

"Yeah. They're okay," Terry replied.

"They checked them at the showroom, before I took the car," Mr. Banks said, signaling to move into the left lane.

A truck roared by, spitting a cloud of exhaust behind it. Greg stared out the front window. His door window was still covered by the new car sticker.

Mr. Banks pulled off the freeway, onto a nearly empty four-lane highway that curved toward the west. The setting sun was a red ball low on the horizon in a charcoal-gray sky.

"Put the pedal to the metal, Dad," Terry urged, sitting up and leaning forward. "Let's see what this car can do."

Mr. Banks obediently pressed his foot on the accelerator. "The cruising speed seems to be about sixty," he said.

"Slow down," Mrs. Banks scolded. "You know the speed limit is fifty-five."

"I'm just testing it," Greg's dad said defensively. "You know. Making sure the transmission doesn't slip or anything."

Greg stared at the glowing speedometer. They were doing seventy now.

"Slow down. I mean it," Mrs. Banks insisted. "You're acting like a crazy teenager."

"That's me!" Mr. Banks replied, laughing. "This is *awesome*!" he said, imitating Terry, ignoring his wife's pleas to slow down.

They roared past a couple of small cars in the right lane. Headlights of cars moving towards them were a bright white blur in the darkening night.

"Hey, Greg, you've been awfully quiet," his mother said. "You feeling okay?"

"Yeah. I'm okay," Greg said softly.

He wished his dad would slow down. He was doing seventy-five now.

"What do you think, Greg?" Mr. Banks asked, steering with his left hand as his right hand searched the dashboard. "Where's the light switch? I should turn on my headlights."

"The car's great," Greg replied, trying to sound enthusiastic. But he couldn't shake away the fear, couldn't get the photo of the mangled car out of his mind.

"Where's that stupid light switch? It's got to be here somewhere," Mr. Banks said.

As he glanced down at the unfamiliar dashboard, the station wagon swerved to the left.

"Dad — look out for that truck!" Greg screamed.

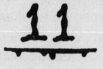

11

Horns blared.

A powerful blast of air swept over the station wagon, like a giant ocean wave pushing it to the side.

Mr. Banks swerved the station wagon to the right.

The truck rumbled past.

"Sorry," Greg's dad said, eyes straight ahead, slowing the car to sixty, fifty-five, fifty . . .

"I *told* you to slow down," Mrs. Banks scolded, shaking her head. "We could've been killed!"

"I was trying to find the lights," he explained. "Oh. Here they are. On the steering wheel." He clicked on the headlights.

"You boys okay?" Mrs. Banks asked, turning to check them out.

"Yeah. Fine," Terry said, sounding a little shaken. The truck would have hit his side of the car.

"I'm okay," Greg said. "Can we go back now?"

"Don't you want to keep going?" Mr. Banks asked, unable to hide his disappointment. "I thought we'd keep going to Santa Clara. Stop and get some ice cream or something."

"Greg's right," Mrs. Banks said softly to her husband. "Enough for tonight, dear. Let's turn around."

"The truck didn't come *that* close," Mr. Banks argued. But he obediently turned off the highway and they headed for home.

Later, safe and sound up in his room, Greg took the photograph out of his dresser and examined it. There was the new station wagon, the driver's side caved in, the windshield shattered.

"Weird," he said aloud, and placed the photo in the secret compartment in his headboard where he had stashed the camera. "Definitely weird."

He pulled the camera out of its hiding place and turned it around in his hands.

I'll try it one more time, he decided.

He walked to his dresser and aimed at the mirror above it.

I'll take a picture of myself in the mirror, he thought.

He raised the camera, then changed his mind. That won't work, he realized. The flash will reflect back and spoil the photo.

Gripping the camera in one hand, he made his way across the hall to Terry's room. His brother was at his desk, typing away on his computer

41

keyboard, his face bathed in the blue light of the monitor screen.

"Terry, can I take your picture?" Greg asked meekly, holding up the camera.

Terry typed some more, then looked up from the screen. "Hey — where'd you get the camera?"

"Uh . . . Shari loaned it to me," Greg told him, thinking quickly. Greg didn't like to lie. But he didn't feel like explaining to Terry how he and his friends had sneaked into the Coffman house and he had made off with the camera.

"So can I take your picture?" Greg asked.

"I'll probably break your camera," Terry joked.

"I think it's already broken," Greg told him. "That's why I want to test it on you."

"Go ahead," Terry said. He stuck out his tongue and crossed his eyes.

Greg snapped the shutter. An undeveloped photo slid out of the slot in front.

"Thanks. See you." Greg headed to the door.

"Hey — don't I get to see it?" Terry called after him.

"If it comes out," Greg said, and hurried across the hall to his room.

He sat down on the edge of the bed. Holding the photo in his lap, he stared at it intently as it developed. The yellows filled in first. Then the reds appeared, followed by shades of blue.

"Whoa," Greg muttered as his brother's face

came into view. "There's something definitely wrong here."

In the photo, Terry's eyes weren't crossed, and his tongue wasn't sticking out. His expression was grim, frightened. He looked very upset.

As the background came into focus, Greg had another surprise. Terry wasn't in his room. He was outdoors. There were trees in the background. And a house.

Greg stared at the house. It looked so familiar.

Was that the house across the street from the playground?

He took one more look at Terry's frightened expression. Then he tucked the photo and the camera into his secret headboard compartment and carefully closed it.

The camera must be broken, he decided, getting changed for bed.

It was the best explanation he could come up with.

Lying in bed, staring up at the shifting shadows on the ceiling, he decided not to think about it anymore.

A broken camera wasn't worth worrying about.

Tuesday afternoon after school, Greg hurried to meet Shari at the playground to watch Bird's Little League game.

It was a warm fall afternoon, the sun high in a

cloudless sky. The outfield grass had been freshly mowed and filled the air with its sharp, sweet smell.

Greg crossed the grass and squinted into the bright sunlight, searching for Shari. Both teams were warming up on the sides of the diamond, yelling and laughing, the sound of balls popping into gloves competing with their loud voices.

A few parents and several kids had come to watch. Some were standing around, some sitting in the low bleachers along the first base line.

Greg spotted Shari behind the backstop and waved to her. "Did you bring the camera?" she asked eagerly, running over to greet him.

He held it up.

"Excellent," she exclaimed, grinning. She reached for it.

"I think it's broken," Greg said, holding on to the camera. "The photos just don't come out right. It's hard to explain."

"Maybe it's not the photos. Maybe it's the photographer," Shari teased.

"Maybe I'll take a photo of you getting a knuckle sandwich," Greg threatened. He raised the camera to his eye and pointed it at her.

"Snap that, and I'll take a picture of you *eating* the camera," Shari threatened playfully. She reached up quickly and pulled the camera from his hand.

"What do you want it for, anyway?" Greg asked, making a halfhearted attempt to grab it back.

Shari held it away from his outstretched hand. "I want to take Bird's picture when he comes to bat. He looks just like an ostrich at the plate."

"I heard that." Bird appeared beside them, pretending to be insulted.

He looked ridiculous in his starched white uniform. The shirt was too big, and the pants were too short. The cap was the only thing that fit. It was blue, with a silver dolphin over the bill and the words: PITTS LANDING DOLPHINS.

"What kind of name is 'Dolphins' for a baseball team?" Greg asked, grabbing the bill and turning the cap backwards on Bird's head.

"All the other caps were taken," Bird answered. "We had a choice between the Zephyrs and the Dolphins. None of us knew what Zephyrs were, so we picked Dolphins."

Shari eyed him up and down. "Maybe you guys should play in your street clothes."

"Thanks for the encouragement," Bird replied. He spotted the camera and took it from her. "Hey, you brought the camera. Does it have film?"

"Yeah. I think so," Greg told him. "Let me see." He reached for the camera, but Bird swung it out of his grasp.

"Hey — are you going to share this thing, Greg?" he asked.

"Huh? What do you mean?" Greg reached again for the camera, and again Bird swung it away from him.

"I mean, we all risked our lives down in that basement getting it, right?" Bird said. "We should all share it."

"Well . . ." Greg hadn't thought about it. "I guess you're right, Bird. But I'm the one who found it. So — "

Shari grabbed the camera out of Bird's hand. "I told Greg to bring it so we could take your picture when you're up."

"As an example of good form?" Bird asked.

"As a *bad* example," Shari said.

"You guys are just jealous," Bird replied, frowning, "because I'm a natural athlete, and you can't cross the street without falling on your face." He turned the cap back around to face the front.

"Hey, Bird — get back here!" one of the coaches called from the playing field.

"I've got to go," Bird said, giving them a quick wave and starting to trot back to his teammates.

"No. Wait. Let me take a fast picture now," Greg said.

Bird stopped, turned around, and struck a pose.

"No. I'll take it," Shari insisted.

She started to raise the camera to her eye, pointing it toward Bird. And as she raised it, Greg grabbed for it.

"Let *me* take it!"

46

And the camera went off. Clicked and then flashed.

An undeveloped photo slid out.

"Hey, why'd you do that?" Shari asked angrily.

"Sorry," Greg said. "I didn't mean to — "

She pulled the photo out and held it in her hand. Greg and Bird came close to watch it develop.

"What the heck is *that*?" Bird cried, staring hard at the small square as the colors brightened and took shape.

"Oh, wow!" Greg cried.

The photo showed Bird sprawled unconscious on his back on the ground, his mouth twisted open, his neck bent at a frightening angle, his eyes shut tight.

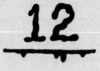

12

"Hey — what's with this stupid camera?" Bird asked, grabbing the snapshot out of Shari's hand. He tilted it from side to side, squinting at it. "It's out of focus or something."

"Weird," Greg said, shaking his head.

"Hey, Bird — get over here!" the Dolphins' coach called.

"Coming!" Bird handed the picture back to Shari and jogged over to his teammates.

Whistles blew. The two teams stopped their practicing and trotted to the benches along the third base line.

"How did this *happen*?" Shari asked Greg, shielding her eyes from the sun with one hand, holding the photo close to her face with the other. "It really looks like Bird is lying on the ground, knocked out or something. But he was standing right in front of us."

"I don't get it. I really don't," Greg replied thoughtfully. "The camera keeps doing that."

Carrying the camera at his side, swinging it by its slender strap, he followed her to a shady spot beside the bleachers.

"Look how his neck is bent," Shari continued. "It's so *awful*."

"There's something definitely wrong with the camera," Greg said. He started to tell her about the snapshot he took of the new station wagon, and the snapshot of his brother Terry. But she interrupted him before he could get the words out.

" — And that picture of Michael. It showed him falling down the stairs before he even fell. It's just so strange."

"I know," Greg agreed.

"Let me see that thing," Shari said and pulled the camera from his hand. "Is there any film left?"

"I can't tell," Greg admitted. "I couldn't find a film counter or anything."

Shari examined the camera closely, rolling it over in her hands. "It doesn't say anywhere. How can you tell if it's loaded or not?"

Greg shrugged.

The baseball game got under way. The Dolphins were the visiting team. The other team, the Cardinals, jogged out to take their positions on the field.

A kid in the bleachers dropped his soda can. It hit the ground and spilled, and the kid started to cry. An old station wagon filled with teenagers cruised by, its radio blaring, its horn honking.

"Where do you put the film in?" Shari asked impatiently.

Greg stepped closer to help her examine it. "Here, I think," he said, pointing. "Doesn't the back come off?"

Shari fiddled with it. "No, I don't think so. Most of these automatic-developing cameras load in the front."

She pulled at the back, but the camera wouldn't open. She tried pulling off the bottom. No better luck. Turning the camera, she tried pulling off the lens. It wouldn't budge.

Greg took the camera from her. "There's no slot or opening in the front."

"Well, what kind of camera is it, anyway?" Shari demanded.

"Uh . . . let's see." Greg studied the front, examined the top of the lens, then turned the camera over and studied the back.

He stared up at her with a surprised look on his face. "There's no brand name. Nothing."

"How can a camera not have a name?" Shari shouted in exasperation. She snatched the camera away from him and examined it closely, squinting her eyes against the bright afternoon sunshine.

Finally, she handed the camera back to him, defeated. "You're right, Greg. No name. No words of any kind. Nothing. What a stupid camera," she added angrily.

"Whoa. Hold on," Greg told her. "It's not my camera, remember? I didn't buy it. I took it from the Coffman house."

"Well, let's at least figure out how to open it up and look inside," Shari said.

The first Dolphin batter popped up to the second baseman. The second batter struck out on three straight swings. The dozen or so spectators shouted encouragement to their team.

The little kid who had dropped his soda continued to cry. Three kids rode by on bikes, waving to friends on the teams, but not stopping to watch.

"I've tried and tried, but I can't figure out how to open it," Greg admitted.

"Give me it," Shari said and grabbed the camera away from him. "There has to be a button or something. There has to be some way of opening it. This is ridiculous."

When she couldn't find a button or lever of any kind, she tried pulling the back off once again, prying it with her fingernails. Then she tried turning the lens, but it wouldn't turn.

"I'm not giving up," she said, gritting her teeth. "I'm not. This camera has to open. It *has* to!"

"Give up. You're going to wreck it," Greg warned, reaching for it.

"Wreck it? How could I wreck it?" Shari demanded. "It has no moving parts. Nothing!"

"This is impossible," Greg said.

Making a disgusted face, she handed the camera to him. "Okay, I give up. Check it out yourself, Greg."

He took the camera, started to raise it to his face, then stopped.

Uttering a low cry of surprise, his mouth dropped open and his eyes gaped straight ahead. Startled, Shari turned to follow his shocked gaze.

"Oh *no!*"

There on the ground a few yards outside the first base line, lay Bird. He was sprawled on his back, his neck bent at an odd and unnatural angle, his eyes shut tight.

13

"Bird!" Shari cried.

Greg's breath caught in his throat. He felt as if he were choking. "Oh!" he finally managed to cry out in a shrill, raspy voice.

Bird didn't move.

Shari and Greg, running side by side at full speed, reached him together.

"Bird?" Shari knelt down beside him. "Bird?"

Bird opened one eye. "Gotcha," he said quietly. The weird half-smile formed on his face, and he exploded in high-pitched laughter.

It took Shari and Greg a while to react. They both stood open-mouthed, gaping at their laughing friend.

Then, his heart beginning to slow to normal, Greg reached down, grabbed Bird with both hands, and pulled him roughly to his feet.

"I'll hold him while you hit him," Greg offered, holding Bird from behind.

"Hey, wait — " Bird protested, struggling to squirm out of Greg's grasp.

"Good plan," Shari said, grinning.

"Ow! Hey — let go! Come on! Let go!" Bird protested, trying unsuccessfully to wrestle free. "Come on! What's your problem? It was a joke, guys."

"Very funny," Shari said, giving Bird a playful punch on the shoulder. "You're a riot, Bird."

Bird finally freed himself with a hard tug and danced away from both of them. "I just wanted to show you how bogus it is to get all worked up about that dumb camera."

"But, Bird — " Greg started.

"It's just broken, that's all," Bird said, brushing blades of recently cut grass off his uniform pants. "You think because it showed Michael falling down those stairs, there's something strange with it. But that's dumb. Real dumb."

"I know it," Greg replied sharply. "But how do you explain it?"

"I told you, man. It's wrecked. Broken. That's it."

"Bird — get over here!" a voice called, and Bird's fielder's glove came flying at his head. He caught it, waved with a grin to Shari and Greg, and jogged to the outfield along with the other members of the Dolphins.

Carrying the camera tightly in one hand, Greg

led the way to the bleachers. He and Shari sat down on the end of the bottom bench.

Some of the spectators had lost interest in the game already and had left. A few kids had taken a baseball off the field and were having their own game of catch behind the bleachers. Across the playground, four or five kids were getting a game of kickball started.

"Bird is such a dork," Greg said, his eyes on the game.

"He scared me to death," Shari exclaimed. "I really thought he was hurt."

"What a clown," Greg muttered.

They watched the game in silence for a while. It wasn't terribly interesting. The Dolphins were losing 12–3 going into the third inning. None of the players were very good.

Greg laughed as a Cardinal batter, a kid from their class named Joe Garden, slugged a ball that sailed out to the field and right over Bird's head.

"That's the third ball that flew over his head!" Greg cried.

"Guess he lost it in the sun!" Shari exclaimed, joining in the laughter.

They both watched Bird's long legs storking after the ball. By the time he managed to catch up with it and heave it towards the diamond, Joe Garden had already rounded the bases and scored.

There were loud *boos* from the bleachers.

The next Cardinal batter stepped to the plate. A few more kids climbed down from the bleachers, having seen enough.

"It's so hot here in the sun," Shari said, shielding her eyes with one hand. "And I've got lots of homework. Want to leave?"

"I just want to see the next inning," Greg said, watching the batter swing and miss. "Bird is coming up next inning. I want to stay and *boo* him."

"What are friends for?" Shari said sarcastically.

It took a long while for the Dolphins to get the third out. The Cardinals batted around their entire order.

Greg's T-shirt was drenched with sweat by the time Bird came to the plate in the top of the fourth.

Despite the loud *booing* from Shari and Greg, Bird managed to punch the ball past the shortstop for a single.

"Lucky hit!" Greg yelled, cupping his hands into a megaphone.

Bird pretended not to hear him. He tossed away his batter's helmet, adjusted his cap, and took a short lead off first base.

The next batter swung at the first pitch and fouled it off.

"Let's go," Shari urged, pulling Greg's arm. "It's too hot. I'm dying of thirst."

"Let's just see if Bird — "

Greg didn't finish his sentence.

The batter hit the next ball hard. It made a loud *thunk* as it left the bat.

A dozen people — players and spectators — cried out as the ball flew across the diamond, a sharp line drive, and slammed into the side of Bird's head with another *thunk*.

Greg watched in horror as the ball bounced off Bird and dribbled away onto the infield grass. Bird's eyes went wide with disbelief, confusion.

He stood frozen in place on the base path for a long moment.

Then both of his hands shot up above his head, and he uttered a shrill cry, long and loud, like the high-pitched whinny of a horse.

His eyes rolled up in his head. He sank to his knees. Uttered another cry, softer this time. Then collapsed, sprawling onto his back, his neck at an unnatural angle, his eyes closed.

He didn't move.

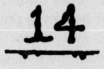

14

In seconds, the two coaches and both teams were running out to the fallen player, huddling over him, forming a tight, hushed circle around him.

Crying, "Bird! Bird!" Shari leapt off the bleachers and began running to the circle of horrified onlookers.

Greg started to follow, but stopped when he saw a familiar figure crossing the street at a full run, waving to him.

"Terry!" Greg cried.

Why was his brother coming to the playground? Why wasn't he at his after-school job at the Dairy Freeze?

"Terry? What's happening?" Greg cried.

Terry stopped, gasping for breath, sweat pouring down his bright red forehead. "I . . . ran . . . all . . . the . . . way," he managed to utter.

"Terry, what's wrong?" A sick feeling crept up from Greg's stomach.

As Terry approached, his face held the same

frightened expression as in the photograph Greg had snapped of him.

The same frightened expression. With the same house behind him across the street.

The snapshot had come true. Just as the snapshot of Bird lying on the ground had come true.

Greg's throat suddenly felt as dry as cotton. He realized that his knees were trembling.

"Terry, what *is* it?" he managed to cry.

"It's Dad," Terry said, putting a heavy hand on Greg's shoulder.

"Huh? Dad?"

"You've got to come home, Greg. Dad — he's been in a bad accident."

"An accident?" Greg's head spun. Terry's words weren't making any sense to him.

"In the new car," Terry explained, again placing a heavy hand on Greg's trembling shoulder. "The new car is totaled. Completely totaled."

"Oh," Greg gasped, feeling weak.

Terry squeezed his shoulder. "Come on. Hurry."

Holding the camera tightly in one hand, Greg began running after his brother.

Reaching the street, he turned back to the playground to see what was happening with Bird.

A large crowd was still huddled around Bird, blocking him from sight.

But — what was that dark shadow behind the bleachers? Greg wondered.

Someone — someone all in black — was hiding back there.

Watching Greg?

"Come *on*!" Terry urged.

Greg stared hard at the bleachers. The dark figure pulled back out of sight.

"Come *on*, Greg!"

"I'm coming!" Greg shouted, and followed his brother toward home.

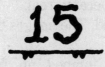

15

The hospital walls were pale green. The uniforms worn by the nurses scurrying through the brightly lit corridors were white. The floor tiles beneath Greg's feet as he hurried with his brother towards their father's room were dark brown with orange specks.

Colors.

All Greg could see were blurs of colors, indistinct shapes.

His sneakers thudded noisily against the hard tile floor. He could barely hear them over the pounding of his heart.

Totaled. The car had been totaled.

Just like in the snapshot.

Greg and Terry turned a corner. The walls in this corridor were pale yellow. Terry's cheeks were red. Two doctors passed by wearing lime-green surgical gowns.

Colors. Only colors.

Greg blinked, tried to see clearly. But it was

all passing by too fast, all too unreal. Even the sharp hospital smell, that unique aroma of rubbing alcohol, stale food, and disinfectant, couldn't make it real for him.

Then the two brothers entered their father's room, and it all became real.

The colors faded. The images became sharp and clear.

Their mother jumped up from the folding chair beside the bed. "Hi, boys." She clenched a wadded-up tissue in her hand. It was obvious that she had been crying. She forced a tight smile on her face, but her eyes were red-rimmed, her cheeks pale and puffy.

Stopping just inside the doorway of the small room, Greg returned his mother's greeting in a soft, choked voice. Then his eyes, focusing clearly now, turned to his father.

Mr. Banks had a mummylike bandage covering his hair. One arm was in a cast. The other lay at his side and had a tube attached just below the wrist, dripping a dark liquid into the arm. The bedsheet was pulled up to his chest.

"Hey — how's it going, guys?" their father asked. His voice sounded fogged in, as if coming from far away.

"Dad — " Terry started.

"He's going to be okay," Mrs. Banks interrupted, seeing the frightened looks on her sons' faces.

"I feel great," Mr. Banks said groggily.

"You don't *look* so great," Greg blurted out, stepping up cautiously to the bed.

"I'm okay. Really," their father insisted. "A few broken bones. That's it." He sighed, then winced from some pain. "I guess I'm lucky."

"You're very lucky," Mrs. Banks agreed quickly.

What's the lucky part? Greg wondered silently to himself. He couldn't take his eyes off the tube stuck into his father's arm.

Again, he thought of the snapshot of the car. It was up in his room at home, tucked into the secret compartment in his headboard.

The snapshot showing the car totaled, the driver's side caved in.

Should he tell them about it?

He couldn't decide.

Would they believe him if he *did* tell them?

"What'd you break, Dad?" Terry asked, sitting down on the radiator in front of the windowsill, shoving his hands into his jeans pockets.

"Your father broke his arm and a few ribs," Mrs. Banks answered quickly. "And he had a slight concussion. The doctors are watching him for internal injuries. But, so far, so good."

"I was lucky," Mr. Banks repeated. He smiled at Greg.

"Dad, I have to tell you about this photo I took," Greg said suddenly, speaking rapidly, his voice

63

trembling with nervousness. "I took a picture of the new car, and — "

"The car is completely wrecked," Mrs. Banks interrupted. Sitting on the edge of the folding chair, she rubbed her fingers, working her wedding ring round and around, something she always did when she was nervous. "I'm glad you boys didn't see it." Her voice caught in her throat. Then she added, "It's a miracle he wasn't hurt any worse."

"This photo — " Greg started again.

"Later," his mother said brusquely. "Okay?" She gave him a meaningful stare.

Greg felt his face grow hot.

This is *important*, he thought.

Then he decided they probably wouldn't believe him, anyway. Who would believe such a crazy story?

"Will we be able to get another new car?" Terry asked.

Mr. Banks nodded carefully. "I have to call the insurance company," he said.

"I'll call them when I get home," Mrs. Banks said. "You don't exactly have a hand free."

Everyone laughed at that, nervous laughter.

"I feel kind of sleepy," Mr. Banks said. His eyes were halfway closed, his voice muffled.

"It's the painkillers the doctors gave you," Mrs. Banks told him. She leaned forward and patted his hand. "Get some sleep. I'll come back in a few hours."

She stood up, still fiddling with her wedding band, and motioned with her head toward the door.

"Bye, Dad," Greg and Terry said in unison.

Their father muttered a reply. They followed their mother out the door.

"What *happened*?" Terry asked as they made their way past a nurses' station, then down the long, pale yellow corridor. "I mean, the accident."

"Some guy ran right through a red light," Mrs. Banks said, her red-rimmed eyes straight ahead. "He plowed right into your father's side of the car. Said his brakes weren't working." She shook her head, tears forming in the corners of her eyes. "I don't know," she said, sighing. "I just don't know what to say. Thank goodness he's going to be okay."

They turned into the green corridor, walking side by side. Several people were waiting patiently for the elevator at the far end of the hall.

Once again, Greg found himself thinking of the snapshots he had taken with the weird camera.

First Michael. Then Terry. Then Bird. Then his father.

All four photos had shown something terrible. Something terrible that hadn't happened yet.

And then all four photos had come true.

Greg felt a chill as the elevator doors opened and the small crowd of people moved forward to squeeze inside.

What was the truth about the camera? he wondered.

Does the camera *show* the future?

Or does it actually *cause* bad things to happen?

16

"Yeah. I know Bird's okay," Greg said into the phone receiver. "I saw him yesterday, remember? He was lucky. Real lucky. He didn't have a concussion or anything."

On the other end of the line — in the house next door — Shari agreed, then repeated her request.

"No, Shari. I really don't want to," Greg replied vehemently.

"Bring it," Shari demanded. "It's *my* birthday."

"I don't want to bring the camera. It's not a good idea. Really," Greg told her.

It was the next weekend. Saturday afternoon. Greg had been nearly out the door, on his way next door to Shari's birthday party, when the phone rang.

"Hi, Greg. Why aren't you on your way to my party?" Shari had asked when he'd run to pick up the receiver.

"Because I'm on the phone with you," Greg had replied dryly.

"Well, bring the camera, okay?"

Greg hadn't looked at the camera, hadn't removed it from its hiding place since his father's accident.

"I don't want to bring it," he insisted, despite Shari's high-pitched demands. "Don't you understand, Shari? I don't want anyone else to get hurt."

"Oh, Greg," she said, talking to him as if he were a three-year-old. "You don't really believe that, do you? You don't really believe that camera can hurt people."

Greg was silent for a moment. "I don't know what I believe," he said finally. "I only know that first, Michael, then, Bird — "

Greg swallowed hard. "And I had a dream, Shari. Last night."

"Huh? What kind of dream?" Shari asked impatiently.

"It was about the camera. I was taking everyone's picture. My whole family — Mom, Dad, and Terry. They were barbecuing. In the back yard. I held up the camera. I kept saying, 'Say Cheese, Say Cheese,' over and over. And when I looked through the viewfinder, they were smiling back at me — but . . . they were skeletons. All of them. Their skin was gone, and — and . . ."

Greg's voice trailed off.

"What a dumb dream," Shari said, laughing.

"But that's why I don't want to bring the camera," Greg insisted. "I think — "

"Bring it, Greg," she interrupted. "It's not your camera, you know. All four of us were in the Coffman house. It belongs to all four of us. Bring it."

"But *why*, Shari?" Greg demanded.

"It'll be a goof, that's all. It takes such weird pictures."

"That's for sure," Greg muttered.

"We don't have anything else to do for my party," Shari told him. "I wanted to rent a video, but my mom says we have to go outdoors. She doesn't want her precious house messed up. So I thought we could take everyone's picture with the weird camera. You know. See what strange things come out."

"Shari, I really don't — "

"Bring it," she ordered. And hung up.

Greg stood for a long time staring at the phone receiver, thinking hard, trying to decide what to do.

Then he replaced the receiver and headed reluctantly up to his room.

With a loud sigh, he pulled the camera from its hiding place in his headboard. "It's Shari's birthday, after all," he said aloud to himself.

His hands were trembling as he picked it up. He realized he was afraid of it.

I shouldn't be doing this, he thought, feeling a heavy knot of dread in the pit of his stomach.

I know I shouldn't be doing this.

17

"How's it going, Bird?" Greg called, making his way across the flagstone patio to Shari's back yard.

"I'm feeling okay," Bird said, slapping his friend a high five. "The only problem is, ever since that ball hit me," Bird continued, frowning, "from time to time I start — *pluuccck cluuuck cluuuuck!* — clucking like a chicken!" He flapped his arms and started strutting across the back yard, clucking at the top of his voice.

"Hey, Bird — go lay an egg!" someone yelled, and everyone laughed.

"Bird's at it again," Michael said, shaking his head. He gave Greg a friendly punch on the shoulder. Michael, his red hair unbrushed as usual, was wearing faded jeans and a flowered Hawaiian sports shirt about three sizes too big for him.

"Where'd you get that shirt?" Greg asked, holding Michael at arm's length by the shoulders to admire it.

70

"In a cereal box," Bird chimed in, still flapping his arms.

"My grandmother gave it to me," Michael said, frowning.

"He made it in home ec," Bird interrupted. One joke was never enough.

"But why did you *wear* it?" Greg asked.

Michael shrugged. "Everything else was dirty."

Bird bent down, picked up a small clump of dirt from the lawn, and rubbed it on the back of Michael's shirt. "Now this one's dirty, too," he declared.

"Hey, you — " Michael reacted with playful anger, grabbing Bird and shoving him into the hedge.

"Did you bring it?"

Hearing Shari's voice, Greg turned towards the house and saw her jogging across the patio in his direction. Her black hair was pulled back in a single braid, and she had on an oversized, silky yellow top that came down over black spandex leggings.

"Did you bring it?" she repeated eagerly. A charm bracelet filled with tiny silver charms — a birthday present — jangled at her wrist.

"Yeah." Greg reluctantly held up the camera.

"Excellent," she declared.

"I really don't want — " Greg started.

"You can take my picture first since it's my birthday," Shari interrupted. "Here. How's this?"

She struck a sophisticated pose, leaning against a tree with her hand behind her head.

Greg obediently raised the camera. "Are you sure you want me to do this, Shari?"

"Yeah. Come on. I want to take everyone's picture."

"But it'll probably come out weird," Greg protested.

"I know," Shari replied impatiently, holding her pose. "That's the fun of it."

"But, Shari — "

"Michael puked on his shirt," he heard Bird telling someone near the hedge.

"I did not!" Michael was screaming.

"You mean it looks like that *naturally*?" Bird asked.

Greg could hear a lot of raucous laughing, all of it at Michael's expense.

"Will you take the picture!" Shari cried, holding on to the slender trunk of the tree.

Greg pointed the lens at her and pressed the button. The camera whirred, and the undeveloped, white square rolled out.

"Hey, are we the only boys invited?" Michael asked, stepping up to Shari.

"Yeah. Just you three," Shari said. "And nine girls."

"Oh, wow." Michael made a face.

"Take Michael's picture next," Shari told Greg.

"No way!" Michael replied quickly, raising his hands as if to shield himself and backing away. "The last time you took my picture with that thing, I fell down the stairs."

Trying to get away, Michael backed right into Nina Blake, one of Shari's friends. She reacted with a squeal of surprise, then gave him a playful shove, and he kept right on backing away.

"Michael, come on. It's *my* party," Shari called.

"What are we going to do? Is this *it*?" Nina demanded from halfway across the yard.

"I thought we'd take everyone's picture and then play a game or something," Shari told her.

"A game?" Bird chimed in. "You mean like Spin the Bottle?"

A few kids laughed.

"Truth or Dare!" Nina suggested.

"Yeah. Truth or Dare!" a couple of other girls called in agreement.

"Oh, no," Greg groaned quietly to himself. Truth or Dare meant a lot of kissing and awkward, embarrassing stunts.

Nine girls and only three boys.

It was going to be *really* embarrassing.

How could Shari *do* this to us? he wondered.

"Well, did it come out?" Shari asked, grabbing his arm. "Let me see."

Greg was so upset about having to play Truth or Dare, he had forgotten about the snapshot developing in his hand. He held it up, and they both examined it.

"Where am I?" Shari asked in surprise. "What were you aiming at? You missed me!"

"Huh?" Greg stared at the snapshot. There was the tree. But no Shari. "Weird! I pointed it right at you. I lined it up carefully," he protested.

"Well, you missed me. I'm not in the shot," Shari replied disgustedly.

"But, Shari — "

"I mean, come *on* — I'm not invisible, Greg. I'm not a vampire or something. I can see my reflection in mirrors. And I do usually show up in photos."

"But, look — " Greg stared hard at the photograph. "There's the tree you were leaning against. You can see the tree trunk clearly. And there's the spot where you were standing."

"But where *am* I?" Shari demanded, jangling her charm bracelet noisily. "Never mind." She grabbed the snapshot from him and tossed it on the grass. "Take another one. Quick."

"Well, okay. But — " Greg was still puzzling over the photo. Why hadn't Shari shown up in it? He bent down, picked it up, and shoved it into his pocket.

"Stand closer this time," she instructed.

Greg moved a few steps closer, carefully centered Shari in the viewfinder, and snapped the

74

picture. A square of film zipped out the front.

Shari walked over and pulled the picture from the camera. "This one better turn out," she said, staring hard at it as the colors began to darken and take form.

"If you really want pictures of everyone, we should get another camera," Greg said, his eyes also locked on the snapshot.

"Hey — I don't *believe* it!" Shari cried.

Again, she was invisible.

The tree photographed clearly, in perfect focus. But Shari was nowhere to be seen.

"You were right. The dumb camera is broken," she said disgustedly, handing the photo to Greg. "Forget it." She turned away from him and called to the others. "Hey, guys — Truth or Dare!"

There were some cheers and some groans.

Shari headed them back to the woods behind her back yard to play. "More privacy," she explained. There was a circular clearing just beyond the trees, a perfect, private place.

The game was just as embarrassing as Greg had imagined. Among the boys, only Bird seemed to be enjoying it. Bird loves dumb stuff like this, Greg thought, with some envy.

Luckily, after little more than half an hour, he heard Mrs. Walker, Shari's mom, calling from the house, summoning them back to cut the birthday cake.

"Aw, too bad," Greg said sarcastically. "Just when the game was getting good."

"We have to get out of the woods, anyway," Bird said, grinning. "Michael's shirt is scaring the squirrels."

Laughing and talking about the game, the kids made their way back to the patio where the pink-and-white birthday cake, candles all lit, was waiting on the round umbrella table.

"I must be a pretty bad mom," Mrs. Walker joked, "allowing you all to go off into the woods by yourselves."

Some of the girls laughed.

Cake knife in her hand, Mrs. Walker looked around. "Where's Shari?"

Everyone turned their eyes to search the back yard. "She was with us in the woods," Nina told Mrs. Walker. "Just a minute ago."

"Hey, Shari!" Bird called, cupping his hands to his mouth as a megaphone. "Earth calling Shari! It's cake time!"

No reply.

No sign of her.

"Did she go in the house?" Greg asked.

Mrs. Walker shook her head. "No. She didn't come by the patio. Is she still in the woods?"

"I'll go check," Bird told her. Calling Shari's name, he ran to the edge of the trees at the back of the yard. Then he disappeared into the trees, still calling.

A few minutes later, Bird emerged, signaling to the others with a shrug.

No sign of her.

They searched the house. The front yard. The woods again.

But Shari had vanished.

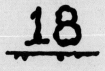

18

Greg sat in the shade with his back against the tree trunk, the camera on the ground at his side, and watched the blue-uniformed policemen.

They covered the back yard and could be seen bending low as they climbed around in the woods. He could hear their voices, but couldn't make out what they were saying. Their faces were intent, bewildered.

More policemen arrived, grim-faced, business-like.

And then, even more dark-uniformed police-men.

Mrs. Walker had called her husband home from a golf game. They sat huddled together on canvas chairs in a corner of the patio. They whispered to each other, their eyes darting across the yard. Holding hands, they looked pale and worried.

Everyone else had left.

On the patio, the table was still set. The birth-day candles had burned all the way down, the blue and red wax melting in hard puddles on the pink-and-white icing, the cake untouched.

"No sign of her," a red-cheeked policeman with a white-blond mustache was telling the Walkers. He pulled off his cap and scratched his head, revealing short, blond hair.

"Did someone . . . take her away?" Mr. Walker asked, still holding his wife's hand.

"No sign of a struggle," the policeman said. "No sign of anything, really."

Mrs. Walker sighed loudly and lowered her head. "I just don't understand it."

There was a long, painful silence.

"We'll keep looking," the policeman said. "I'm sure we'll find . . . something."

He turned and headed toward the woods.

"Oh. Hi." He stopped in front of Greg, staring down at him as if seeing him for the first time. "You still here, son? All the other guests have gone home." He pushed his hair back and replaced his cap.

"Yeah, I know," Greg replied solemnly, lifting the camera into his lap.

"I'm Officer Riddick," he said.

"Yeah, I know," Greg repeated softly.

"How come you didn't go home after we talked with you, like the others?" Riddick asked.

"I'm just upset, I guess," Greg told him. "I mean, Shari's a good friend, you know?" He cleared his throat, which felt dry and tight. "Besides, I live right over there." He gestured with his head to his house next door.

"Well, you might as well go home, son," Riddick said, turning his eyes to the woods with a frown. "This search could take a long time. We haven't found a thing back there yet."

"I know," Greg replied, rubbing his hand against the back of the camera.

And I know that this camera is the reason Shari is missing, he thought, feeling miserable and frightened.

"One minute she was there. The next minute she was gone," the policeman said, studying Greg's face as if looking for answers there.

"Yeah," Greg replied. "It's so weird."

It's weirder than anyone knows, Greg thought.

The camera made her invisible. The camera did it.

First, she vanished from the snapshot.

Then she vanished in real life.

The camera did it to her. I don't know how. But it did.

"Do you have something more to tell me?" Riddick asked, hands resting on his hips, his right hand just above the worn brown holster that carried his pistol. "Did you see something? Something that might give us a clue, help us out? Something you didn't remember to tell me before?"

Should I tell him? Greg wondered.

If I tell him about the camera, he'll ask where I got it. And I'll have to tell him that I got it in the Coffman house. And we'll all get in trouble for breaking in there.

But — big deal. Shari is missing. Gone. Vanished. That's a lot more important.

I should tell him, Greg decided.

But then he hesitated. If I tell him, he won't believe me.

If I tell him, how will it help bring Shari back?

"You look very troubled," Riddick said, squatting down next to Greg in the shade. "What's your name again?"

"Greg. Greg Banks."

"Well, you look very troubled, Greg," the policeman repeated softly. "Why don't you tell me what's bothering you? Why don't you tell me what's on your mind? I think it'll make you feel a lot better."

Greg took a deep breath and glanced up to the patio. Mrs. Walker had covered her face with her hands. Her husband was leaning over her, trying to comfort her.

"Well . . ." Greg started.

"Go ahead, son," Riddick urged softly. "Do you know where Shari is?"

"It's this camera," Greg blurted out. He could suddenly feel the blood throbbing against his temples.

He took a deep breath and then continued. "You see, this camera is weird."

"What do you mean?" Riddick asked quietly.

Greg took another deep breath. "I took Shari's picture. Before. When I first arrived. I took two pictures. And she was invisible. In both of them. See?"

Riddick closed his eyes, then opened them. "No. I don't understand."

"Shari was invisible in the picture. Everything else was there. But she wasn't. She had vanished, see. And, then, later, she vanished for real. The camera — it predicts the future, I guess. Or it makes bad things happen." Greg raised the camera, attempting to hand it to the policeman.

Riddick made no attempt to take it. He just stared hard at Greg, his eyes narrowing, his expression hardening.

Greg felt a sudden stab of fear.

Oh, no, he thought. Why is he looking at me like that?

What is he going to do?

19

Greg continued to hold the camera out to the policeman.

But Riddick quickly climbed to his feet. "The camera makes bad things happen?" His eyes burned into Greg's.

"Yes," Greg told him. "It isn't my camera, see? And every time I take a picture — "

"Son, that's enough," Riddick said gently. He reached down and rested a hand on Greg's trembling shoulder. "I think you're very upset, Greg," he said, his voice almost a whisper. "I don't blame you. This is very upsetting for everyone."

"But it's *true* — " Greg started to insist.

"I'm going to ask that officer over there," Riddick said, pointing, "to take you home now. And I'm going to have him tell your parents that you've been through a very frightening experience."

I *knew* he wouldn't believe me, Greg thought angrily.

How could I have been so stupid?

Now he thinks I'm some kind of a nut case.

Riddick called to a policeman at the side of the house near the hedge.

"No, that's okay," Greg said, quickly pulling himself up, cradling the camera in his hand. "I can make it home okay."

Riddick eyed him suspiciously. "You sure?"

"Yeah. I can walk by myself."

"If you have anything to tell me later," Riddick said, lowering his gaze to the camera, "just call the station, okay?"

"Okay," Greg replied, walking slowly towards the front of the house.

"Don't worry, Greg. We'll do our best," Riddick called after him. "We'll find her. Put the camera away and try to get some rest, okay?"

"Okay," Greg muttered.

He hurried past the Walkers, who were still huddled together under the umbrella on the patio.

Why was I so stupid? he asked himself as he walked home. Why did I expect that policeman to believe such a weird story?

I'm not even sure I believe it myself.

A few minutes later, he pulled open the back screen door and entered his kitchen. "Anybody home?"

No reply.

He headed through the back hall towards the living room. "Anyone home?"

No one.

Terry was at work. His mother must have been visiting his dad at the hospital.

Greg felt bad. He really didn't feel like being alone now. He really wanted to tell them about what had happened to Shari. He really wanted to talk to them.

Still cradling the camera, he climbed the stairs to his room.

He stopped in the doorway, blinked twice, then uttered a cry of horror.

His books were scattered all over the floor. The covers had been pulled off his bed. His desk drawers were all open, their contents strewn around the room. The desk lamp was on its side on the floor. All of his clothes had been pulled from the dresser and his closet and tossed everywhere.

Someone had been in Greg's room — and had turned it upside down!

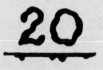

20

Who would do this? Greg asked himself, staring in horror at his ransacked room.

Who would tear my room apart like this?

He realized that he knew the answer. He knew who would do it, who *had* done it.

Someone looking for the camera.

Someone desperate to get the camera back.

Spidey?

The creepy guy who dressed all in black was living in the Coffman house. Was he the owner of the camera?

Yes, Greg knew, Spidey had done it.

Spidey had been watching Greg, spying on Greg from behind the bleachers at the Little League game.

He knew that Greg had his camera. *And he knew where Greg lived.*

That thought was the most chilling of all.

He knew where Greg lived.

Greg turned away from the chaos in his room,

leaned against the wall of the hallway, and closed his eyes.

He pictured Spidey, the dark figure creeping along so evilly on his spindly legs. He pictured him inside the house, Greg's house. Inside Greg's room.

He was here, thought Greg. He pawed through all my things. He wrecked my room.

Greg stepped back into his room. He felt all mixed up. He felt like shouting angrily and crying for help all at once.

But he was all alone. No one to hear him. No one to help him.

What now? he wondered. What now?

Suddenly, leaning against the doorframe, staring at his ransacked room, he knew what he had to do.

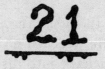

21

"Hey, Bird, it's me."

Greg held the receiver in one hand and wiped the sweat off his forehead with the other. He'd never worked so hard — or so fast — in all his life.

"Did they find Shari?" Bird asked eagerly.

"I haven't heard. I don't think so," Greg said, his eyes surveying his room. Almost back to normal.

He had put everything back, cleaned and straightened. His parents would never guess.

"Listen, Bird, I'm not calling about that," Greg said, speaking rapidly into the phone. "Call Michael for me, okay? Meet me at the playground. By the baseball diamond."

"When? Now?" Bird asked, sounding confused.

"Yeah," Greg told him. "We have to meet. It's important."

"It's almost dinnertime," Bird protested. "I don't know if my parents — "

"It's important," Greg repeated impatiently. "I've got to see you guys. Okay?"

"Well . . . maybe I can sneak out for a few minutes," Bird said, lowering his voice. And then Greg heard him shout to his mother: "It's no one, Ma! I'm talking to no one!"

Boy, *that's* quick thinking! Greg thought sarcastically. He's a worse liar than I am!

And then he heard Bird call to his mom: "I *know* I'm on the phone. But I'm not talking to anyone. It's only Greg."

Thanks a lot, pal, Greg thought.

"I gotta go," Bird said.

"Get Michael, okay?" Greg urged.

"Yeah. Okay. See you." He hung up.

Greg replaced the receiver, then listened for his mother. Silence downstairs. She still wasn't home. She didn't know about Shari, Greg realized. He knew she and his dad were going to be very upset.

Very upset.

Almost as upset as he was.

Thinking about his missing friend, he went to his bedroom window and looked down on her yard next door. It was deserted now.

The policemen had all left. Shari's shaken parents must have gone inside.

A squirrel sat under the wide shade of the big tree, gnawing furiously at an acorn, another acorn at his feet.

In the corner of the window, Greg could see the birthday cake, still sitting forlornly on the deserted table, the places all set, the decorations still standing.

A birthday party for ghosts.

Greg shuddered.

"Shari is alive," he said aloud. "They'll find her. She's alive."

He knew what he had to do now.

Forcing himself away from the window, he hurried to meet his two friends.

22

"No way," Bird said heatedly, leaning against the bleacher bench. "Have you gone totally bananas?"

Swinging the camera by its cord, Greg turned hopefully to Michael. But Michael avoided Greg's stare. "I'm with Bird," he said, his eyes on the camera.

Since it was just about dinnertime, the playground was nearly deserted. A few little kids were on the swings at the other end. Two kids were riding their bikes round and around the soccer field.

"I thought maybe you guys would come with me," Greg said, disappointed. He kicked up a clump of grass with his sneaker. "I have to return this thing," he continued, raising the camera. "I know it's what I have to do. I have to put it back where I found it."

"No way," Bird repeated, shaking his head. "I'm not going back to the Coffman house. Once was enough."

"Chicken?" Greg asked angrily.

"Yeah," Bird quickly admitted.

"You don't have to take it back," Michael argued. He pulled himself up the side of the bleachers, climbed onto the third deck of seats, then lowered himself to the ground.

"What do you mean?" Greg asked impatiently, kicking at the grass.

"Just toss it, Greg," Michael urged, making a throwing motion with one hand. "Heave it. Throw it in the trash somewhere."

"Yeah. Or leave it right here," Bird suggested. He reached for the camera. "Give it to me. I'll hide it under the seats."

"You don't understand," Greg said, swinging the camera out of Bird's reach. "Throwing it away won't do any good."

"Why not?" Bird asked, making another swipe for the camera.

"Spidey'll just come back for it," Greg told him heatedly. "He'll come back to my room looking for it. He'll come after me. I know it."

"But what if we get caught taking it back?" Michael asked.

"Yeah. What if Spidey's there in the Coffman house, and he catches us?" Bird said.

"You don't understand," Greg cried. "He knows where I live! He was in my house. He was in my *room*! He wants his camera back, and — "

"Here. Give it to me," Bird said. "We don't have

to go back to that house. He can find it. Right here."

He grabbed again for the camera.

Greg held tightly to the strap and tried to tug it away.

But Bird grabbed the side of the camera.

"No!" Greg cried out as it flashed. And whirred.

A square of film slid out.

"No!" Greg cried to Bird, horrified, staring at the white square as it started to develop. "You took *my* picture!"

His hand trembling, he pulled the snapshot from the camera.

What would it show?

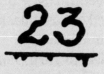

23

"Sorry," Bird said. "I didn't mean to — "

Before he could finish his sentence, a voice interrupted from behind the bleachers. "Hey — what've you got there?"

Greg looked up from the developing snapshot in surprise. Two tough-looking boys stepped out of the shadows, their expressions hard, their eyes on the camera.

He recognized them immediately — Joey Ferris and Mickey Ward — two ninth-graders who hung out together, always swaggering around, acting tough, picking on kids younger than them.

Their specialty was taking kids' bikes, riding off on them, and dumping them somewhere. There was a rumor around school that Mickey had once beaten up a kid so badly that the kid was crippled for life. But Greg believed Mickey made up that rumor and spread it himself.

Both boys were big for their age. Neither of them did very well in school. And even though they were always stealing bikes and skateboards, and terrorizing little kids, and getting into fights, neither of them ever seemed to get into serious trouble.

Joey had short blond hair, slicked straight up, and wore a diamondlike stud in one ear. Mickey had a round, red face full of pimples, stringy black hair down to his shoulders, and was working a toothpick between his teeth. Both boys were wearing heavy metal T-shirts and jeans.

"Hey, I've gotta get home," Bird said quickly, half-stepping, half-dancing away from the bleachers.

"Me, too," Michael said, unable to keep the fear from showing on his face.

Greg tucked the snapshot into his jeans pocket.

"Hey, you found my camera," Joey said, grabbing it out of Greg's hand. His small, gray eyes burned into Greg's as if searching for a reaction. "Thanks, man."

"Give it back, Joey," Greg said with a sigh.

"Yeah. Don't take that camera," Mickey told his friend, a smile spreading over his round face. "It's *mine*!" He wrestled the camera away from Joey.

"Give it back," Greg insisted angrily, reaching out his hand. Then he softened his tone. "Come on, guys. It isn't mine."

"I *know* it isn't yours," Mickey said, grinning. "Because it's *mine*!"

"I have to give it back to the owner," Greg told him, trying not to whine, but hearing his voice edge up.

"No, you don't. I'm the owner now," Mickey insisted.

"Haven't you ever heard of finders keepers?" Joey asked, leaning over Greg menacingly. He was about six inches taller than Greg, and a lot more muscular.

"Hey, let him have the thing," Michael whispered in Greg's ear. "You wanted to get rid of it — right?"

"No!" Greg protested.

"What's your problem, Freckle Face?" Joey asked Michael, eyeing Michael up and down.

"No problem," Michael said meekly.

"Hey — say cheese!" Mickey aimed the camera at Joey.

"Don't do it," Bird interrupted, waving his hands frantically.

"Why not?" Joey demanded.

"Because your face will break the camera," Bird said, laughing.

"You're real funny," Joey said sarcastically, narrowing his eyes threateningly, hardening his features. "You want that stupid smile to be permanent?" He raised a big fist.

"I know this kid," Mickey told Joey, pointing at Bird. "Thinks he's hot stuff."

Both boys stared hard at Bird, trying to scare him.

Bird swallowed hard. He took a step back, bumping into the bleachers. "No, I don't," he said softly. "I don't think I'm hot stuff."

"He looks like something I stepped in yesterday," Joey said.

He and Mickey cracked up, laughing high-pitched hyena laughs and slapping each other high fives.

"Listen, guys. I really need the camera back," Greg said, reaching out a hand to take it. "It isn't any good, anyway. It's broken. And it doesn't belong to me."

"Yeah, that's right. It's broken," Michael added, nodding his head.

"Yeah. Right," Mickey said sarcastically. "Let's just see." He raised the camera again and pointed it at Joey.

"Really, guys. I need it back," Greg said desperately.

If they took a picture with the camera, Greg realized, they might discover its secret. That its snapshots showed the future, showed only bad things happening to people. That the camera was evil. Maybe it even *caused* evil.

"Say cheese," Mickey instructed Joey.

"Just snap the stupid thing!" Joey replied impatiently.

No, Greg thought. I can't let this happen. I've got to return the camera to the Coffman house, to Spidey.

Impulsively, Greg leapt forward. With a cry, he snatched the camera away from Mickey's face.

"Hey — " Mickey reacted in surprise.

"Let's *go!*" Greg shouted to Bird and Michael.

And without another word, the three friends turned and began running across the deserted playground towards their homes.

His heart thudding in his chest, Greg gripped the camera tightly and ran as fast as he could, his sneakers pounding over the dry grass.

They're going to catch us, Greg thought, panting loudly now as he raced toward the street. They're going to catch us and pound us. They're going to take back the camera. We're dead meat. Dead meat.

Greg and his friends didn't turn around until they were across the street. Breathing noisily, they looked back — and cried out in relieved surprise.

Joey and Mickey hadn't budged from beside the bleachers. They hadn't chased after them. They were leaning against the bleachers, laughing.

"Catch you later, guys!" Joey called after them.

"Yeah. Later," Mickey repeated.

They both burst out laughing again, as if they had said something hilarious.

"That was close," Michael said, still breathing hard.

"They mean it," Bird said, looking very troubled. "They'll catch us later. We're history."

"Tough talk. They're just a lot of hot air," Greg insisted.

"Oh, yeah?" Michael cried. "Then why did we run like that?"

"Because we're late for dinner," Bird joked. "See you guys. I'm gonna catch it if I don't hurry."

"But the camera — " Greg protested, still gripping it tightly in one hand.

"It's too late," Michael said, nervously raking a hand back through his red hair.

"Yeah. We'll have to do it tomorrow or something," Bird agreed.

"Then you guys will come with me?" Greg asked eagerly.

"Uh . . . I've gotta go," Bird said without answering.

"Me, too," Michael said quickly, avoiding Greg's stare.

All three of them turned their eyes back to the playground. Joey and Mickey had disappeared. Probably off to terrorize some other kids.

"Later," Bird said, slapping Greg on the shoulder as he headed away. The three friends split up, running in different directions across lawns and driveways, heading home.

Greg had run all the way to his front yard before he remembered the snapshot he had shoved into his jeans pocket.

He stopped in the driveway and pulled it out.

The sun was lowering behind the garage. He held the snapshot up close to his face to see it clearly.

"Oh, no!" he cried. "I don't believe it!"

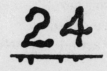

24

"This is *impossible!*" Greg cried aloud, gaping at the snapshot in his trembling hand.

How had Shari gotten into the photo?

It had been taken a few minutes before, in front of the bleachers on the playground.

But there was Shari, standing close beside Greg.

His hand trembling, his mouth hanging open in disbelief, Greg goggled at the photo.

It was very clear, very sharp. There they were on the playground. He could see the baseball diamond in the background.

And there they were. Greg and Shari.

Shari standing so clear, so sharp — right next to him.

And they were both staring straight ahead, their eyes wide, their mouths open, their expressions frozen in horror as a large shadow covered them both.

"Shari?" Greg cried, lowering the snapshot and

darting his eyes over the front yard. "Are you here? Can you hear me?"

He listened.

Silence.

He tried again.

"Shari? Are you here?"

"Greg!" a voice called.

Uttering a startled cry, Greg spun around. "Huh?"

"Greg!" the voice repeated. It took him a while to realize that it was his mother, calling to him from the front door.

"Oh. Hi, Mom." Feeling dazed, he slid the snapshot back into his jeans pocket.

"Where've you been?" his mother asked as he made his way to the door. "I heard about Shari. I've been so upset. I didn't know where you were."

"Sorry, Mom," Greg said, kissing her on the cheek. "I — I should've left a note."

He stepped into the house, feeling strange and out-of-sorts, sad and confused and frightened, all at the same time.

Two days later, on a day of high, gray clouds, the air hot and smoggy, Greg paced back and forth in his room after school.

The house was empty except for him. Terry had gone off a few hours before to his after-school job at the Dairy Freeze. Mrs. Banks had driven to the hospital to pick up Greg's dad, who was finally coming home.

Greg knew he should be happy about his dad's return. But there were still too many things troubling him, tugging at his mind.

Frightening him.

For one thing, Shari still hadn't been found.

The police were completely baffled. Their new theory was that she'd been kidnapped.

Her frantic, grieving parents waited home by the phone. But no kidnappers called to demand a ransom.

There were no clues of any kind.

Nothing to do but wait. And hope.

As the days passed, Greg felt more and more guilty. He was sure Shari hadn't been kidnapped. He knew that somehow, the camera had made her disappear.

But he couldn't tell anyone else what he believed.

No one would believe him. Anyone he tried to tell the story to would think he was crazy.

Cameras can't be evil, after all.

Cameras can't make people fall down stairs. Or crash their cars.

Or vanish from sight.

Cameras can only record what they see.

Greg stared out of his window, pressing his forehead against the glass, looking down on

Shari's back yard. "Shari — where *are* you?" he asked aloud, staring at the tree where she had posed.

The camera was still hidden in the secret compartment in his headboard. Neither Bird nor Michael would agree to help Greg return it to the Coffman house.

Besides, Greg had decided to hold on to it a while longer, in case he needed it as proof.

In case he decided to confide his fears about it to someone.

In case . . .

His other fear was that Spidey would come back, back to Greg's room, back for the camera.

So much to be frightened about.

He pushed himself away from the window. He had spent so much time in the past couple of days staring down at Shari's empty back yard.

Thinking. Thinking.

With a sigh, he reached into the headboard and pulled out two of the snapshots he had hidden in there along with the camera.

The two snapshots were the ones taken the past Saturday at Shari's birthday party. Holding one in each hand, Greg stared at them, hoping he could see something new, something he hadn't noticed before.

But the photos hadn't changed. They still showed her tree, her back yard, green in the sunlight. And no Shari. No one where Shari had been standing. As if the lens had penetrated right through her.

Staring at the photos, Greg let out a cry of anguish.

If only he had never gone into the Coffman house.

If only he had never stolen the camera.

If only he had never taken any photos with it.

If only . . . if only . . . if only . . .

Before he realized what he was doing, he was ripping the two snapshots into tiny pieces.

Panting loudly, his chest heaving, he tore at the snapshots and let the pieces fall to the floor.

When he had ripped them both into tiny shards of paper, he flung himself facedown on his bed and closed his eyes, waiting for his heart to stop pounding, waiting for the heavy feeling of guilt and horror to lift.

Two hours later, the phone by his bed rang.

It was Shari.

25

"Shari — is it really you?" Greg shouted into the phone.

"Yeah. It's me!" She sounded as surprised as he did.

"But how? I mean — " His mind was racing. He didn't know what to say.

"Your guess is as good as mine," Shari told him. And then she said, "Hold on a minute." And he heard her step away from the phone to talk to her mother. "Mom — stop crying already. Mom — it's really me. I'm home."

A few seconds later, she came back on the line. "I've been home for two hours, and Mom's still crying and carrying on."

"I feel like crying, too," Greg admitted. "I — I just can't believe it! Shari, where *were* you?"

The line was silent for a long moment. "I don't know," she answered finally.

"Huh?"

"I really don't. It was just so weird, Greg. One

minute, there I was at my birthday party. The next minute, I was standing in front of my house. And it was two days later. But I don't remember being away. Or being anywhere else. I don't remember anything at all."

"You don't remember going away? Or coming back?" Greg asked.

"No. Nothing," Shari said, her voice trembling.

"Shari, those pictures I took of you — remember? With the weird camera? You were invisible in them — "

"And then I disappeared," she said, finishing his thought.

"Shari, do you think — ?"

"I don't know," she replied quickly. "I — I have to get off now. The police are here. They want to question me. What am I going to tell them? They're going to think I had amnesia or flipped out or something."

"I — I don't know," Greg said, completely bewildered. "We have to talk. The camera — "

"I can't now," she told him. "Maybe tomorrow. Okay?" She called to her mother that she was coming. "Bye, Greg. See you." And then she hung up.

Greg replaced the receiver, but sat on the edge of his bed staring at the phone for a long time.

Shari was back.

She'd been back about two hours.

Two hours. Two hours. Two hours.

He turned his eyes to the clock radio beside the phone.

Just two hours before, he had ripped up the two snapshots of an invisible Shari.

His mind whirred with wild ideas, insane ideas.

Had he brought Shari back by ripping up the photos?

Did this mean that the camera *caused* her to disappear? That the camera *caused* all of the terrible things that showed up in its snapshots?

Greg stared at the phone for a long time, thinking hard.

He knew what he had to do. He had to talk to Shari. And he had to return the camera.

He met Shari on the playground the next afternoon. The sun floated high in a cloudless sky. Eight or nine kids were engaged in a noisy brawl of a soccer game, running one way, then the other across the outfield of the baseball diamond.

"Hey — you look like *you*!" Greg exclaimed as Shari came jogging up to where he stood beside the bleachers. He pinched her arm. "Yeah. It's you, okay."

She didn't smile. "I feel fine," she told him, rubbing her arm. "Just confused. And tired. The police asked me questions for hours. And when they finally went away, my parents started in."

"Sorry," Greg said quietly, staring down at his sneakers.

"I think Mom and Dad believe somehow it's my fault that I disappeared," Shari said, resting her back against the side of the bleachers, shaking her head.

"It's the camera's fault," Greg muttered. He raised his eyes to hers. "The camera is evil."

Shari shrugged. "Maybe. I don't know what to think. I really don't."

He showed her the snapshot, the one showing the two of them on the playground staring in horror as a shadow crept over them.

"How weird," Shari exclaimed, studying it hard.

"I want to take the camera back to the Coffman house," Greg said heatedly. "I can go home and get it now. Will you help me? Will you come with me?"

Shari started to reply, but stopped.

They both saw the dark shadow move, sliding toward them quickly, silently, over the grass.

And then they saw the man dressed all in black, his spindly legs pumping hard as he came at them.

Spidey!

Greg grabbed Shari's hand, frozen in fear.

He and Shari gaped in terror as Spidey's slithering shadow crept over them.

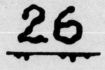

26

Greg had a shudder of recognition. He knew the snapshot had just come true.

As the dark figure of Spidey moved toward them like a black tarantula, Greg pulled Shari's hand. "Run!" he cried in a shrill voice he didn't recognize.

He didn't have to say it. They were both running now, gasping as they ran across the grass toward the street. Their sneakers thudded loudly on the ground as they reached the sidewalk and kept running.

Greg turned to see Spidey closing the gap. "He's catching up!" he managed to cry to Shari, who was a few steps ahead of him.

Spidey, his face still hidden in the shadows of his black baseball cap, moved with startling speed, his long legs kicking high as he pursued them.

"He's going to catch us!" Greg cried, feeling as

if his chest were about to burst. "*He's* . . . too . . . fast!"

Spidey moved even closer, his shadow scuttling over the grass.

Closer.

When the car horn honked, Greg screamed.

He and Shari stopped short.

The horn blasted out again.

Greg turned to see a familiar young man inside a small hatchback. It was Jerry Norman, who lived across the street. Jerry lowered his car window. "Is this man chasing you?" he asked excitedly. Without waiting for an answer, he backed the car towards Spidey. "I'm calling the cops, mister!"

Spidey didn't reply. Instead, he turned and darted across the street.

"I'm warning you — " Jerry called after him.

But Spidey had disappeared behind a tall hedge.

"Are you kids okay?" Greg's neighbor demanded.

"Yeah. Fine," Greg managed to reply, still breathing hard, his chest heaving.

"We're okay. Thanks, Jerry," Shari said.

"I've seen that guy around the neighborhood," the young man said, staring through the windshield at the tall hedge. "Never thought he was dangerous. You kids want me to call the police?"

"No. It's okay," Greg replied.

As soon as I give him back his camera, he'll stop chasing us, Greg thought.

"Well, be careful — okay?" Jerry said. "You need a lift home or anything?" He studied their faces as if trying to determine how frightened and upset they were.

Greg and Shari both shook their heads. "We'll be okay," Greg said. "Thanks."

Jerry warned them once again to be careful, then drove off, his tires squealing as he turned the corner.

"That was close," Shari said, her eyes on the hedge. "Why was Spidey chasing us?"

"He thought I had the camera. He wants it back," Greg told her. "Meet me tomorrow, okay? In front of the Coffman house. Help me put it back?"

Shari stared at him without replying, her expression thoughtful, wary.

"We're going to be in danger — all of us — until we put that camera back," Greg insisted.

"Okay," Shari said quietly. "Tomorrow."

27

Something scurried through the tall weeds of the unmowed front lawn. "What *was* that?" Shari cried, whispering even though no one else was in sight. "It was too big to be a squirrel."

She lingered behind Greg, who stopped to look up at the Coffman house. "Maybe it was a racoon or something," Greg told her. He gripped the camera tightly in both hands.

It was a little after three o'clock the next afternoon, a hazy, overcast day. Mountains of dark clouds threatening rain were rolling across the sky, stretching behind the house, casting it in shadow.

"It's going to storm," Shari said, staying close behind Greg. "Let's get this over with and go home."

"Good idea," he said, glancing up at the heavy sky.

Thunder rumbled in the distance, a low roar.

The old trees that dotted the front yard whispered and shook.

"We can't just run inside," Greg told her, watching the sky darken. "First we have to make sure Spidey isn't there."

Making their way quickly through the tall grass and weeds, they stopped at the living room window and peered in. Thunder rumbled, low and long, in the distance. Greg thought he saw another creature scuttle through the weeds around the corner of the house.

"It's too dark in there. I can't see a thing," Shari complained.

"Let's check out the basement," Greg suggested. "That's where Spidey hangs out, remember?"

The sky darkened to an eerie gray-green as they made their way to the back of the house and dropped to their knees to peer down through the basement windows at ground level.

Squinting through the dust-covered window-panes they could see the makeshift, plywood table Spidey had made, the wardrobe against the wall, its doors still open, the colorful, old clothing spilling out, the empty frozen food boxes scattered on the floor.

"No sign of him," Greg whispered, cradling the camera in his arm as if it might try to escape from him if he didn't hold it tightly. "Let's get moving."

"Are — are you sure?" Shari stammered. She

wanted to be brave. But the thought that she had disappeared for two days — completely *vanished*, most likely because of the camera — that frightening thought lingered in her mind.

Michael and Bird were chicken, she thought. But maybe they were the smart ones.

She wished this were over. All over.

A few seconds later, Greg and Shari pushed open the front door. They stepped into the darkness of the front hall. And stopped.

And listened.

And then they both jumped at the sound of the loud, sudden crash directly behind them.

28

Shari was the first to regain her voice. "It's just the door!" she cried. "The wind — "

A gust of wind had made the front door slam.

"Let's get this over with," Greg whispered, badly shaken.

"We never should've broken into this house in the first place," Shari whispered as they made their way on tiptoe, step by creaking step, down the dark hallway toward the basement stairs.

"It's a little late for that," Greg replied sharply.

Pulling open the door to the basement steps, he stopped again. "What's that banging sound upstairs?"

Shari's features tightened in fear as she heard it, too, a repeated, almost rhythmic banging.

"Shutters?" Greg suggested.

"Yeah," she quickly agreed, breathing a sigh of relief. "A lot of the shutters are loose, remember?"

The entire house seemed to groan.

Thunder rumbled outside, closer now.

They stepped onto the landing, then waited for their eyes to adjust to the darkness.

"Couldn't we just leave the camera up here, and run?" Shari asked, more of a plea than a question.

"No. I want to put it back," Greg insisted.

"But, Greg — " She tugged at his arm as he started down the stairs.

"No!" He pulled out of her grasp. "He was in my *room*, Shari! He tore everything apart, looking for it. I want him to find it where it belongs. If he doesn't find it, he'll come back to my house. I *know* he will!"

"Okay, okay. Let's just hurry."

It was brighter in the basement, gray light seeping down from the four ground-level windows. Outside, the wind swirled and pushed against the windowpanes. A pale flash of lightning made shadows flicker against the basement wall. The old house groaned as if unhappy about the storm.

"What was *that*? Footsteps?" Shari stopped halfway across the basement and listened.

"It's just the house," Greg insisted. But his quivering voice revealed that he was as frightened as his companion, and he stopped to listen, too.

Bang. Bang. Bang.

The shutter high above them continued its rhythmic pounding.

"Where did you find the camera, anyway?" Shari whispered, following Greg to the far wall across from the enormous furnace with its cob-webbed ducts sprouting up like pale tree limbs.

"Over here," Greg told her. He stepped up to the worktable and reached for the vise clamped on the edge. "When I turned the vise, a door opened up. Some kind of hidden shelf. That's where the camera — "

He cranked the handle of the vise.

Once again, the door to the secret shelf popped open.

"Good," he whispered excitedly. He flashed Shari a smile.

He shoved the camera onto the shelf, tucking the carrying strap under it. Then he pushed the door closed. "We're out of here."

He felt so much better. So relieved. So much *lighter*.

The house groaned and creaked. Greg didn't care.

Another flash of lightning, brighter this time, like a camera flash, sent shadows flickering on the wall.

"Come on," he whispered. But Shari was already ahead of him, making her way carefully over the food cartons strewn everywhere, hurrying towards the steps.

They were halfway up the stairs, Greg one step behind Shari, when, above them, Spidey stepped silently into view on the landing, blocking their escape.

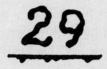

29

Greg blinked and shook his head, as if he could shake away the image of the figure that stared darkly down at him.

"No!" Shari cried out, and fell back against Greg.

He grabbed for the railing, forgetting that it had fallen under Michael's weight during their first unfortunate visit to the house. Luckily, Shari regained her balance before toppling them both down the stairs.

Lightning flashed behind them, sending a flash of white light across the stairway. But the unmoving figure on the landing above them remained shrouded in darkness.

"Let us go!" Greg finally managed to cry, finding his voice.

"Yeah. We returned your camera!" Shari added, sounding shrill and frightened.

Spidey didn't reply. Instead, he took a step towards them, onto the first step. And then he descended another step.

Nearly stumbling again, Greg and Shari backed down to the basement floor.

The wooden stairs squeaked in protest as the dark figure stepped slowly, steadily, down. As he reached the basement floor, a crackling bolt of lightning cast a blue light over him, and Greg and Shari saw his face for the first time.

In the brief flash of color, they saw that he was old, older than they had imagined. That his eyes were small and round like dark marbles. That his mouth was small, too, pursed in a tight, menacing grimace.

"We returned the camera," Shari said, staring in fear as Spidey crept closer. "Can't we go now? Please?"

"Let me see," Spidey said. His voice was younger than his face, warmer than his eyes. "Come."

They hesitated. But he gave them no choice.

Ushering them back across the cluttered floor to the worktable, he wrapped his large, spidery hand over the vise and turned the handle. The door opened. He pulled out the camera and held it close to his face to examine it.

"You shouldn't have taken it," he told them, speaking softly, turning the camera in his hands.

"We're sorry," Shari said quickly.

"Can we go now?" Greg asked, edging towards the stairs.

"It's not an ordinary camera," Spidey said, raising his small eyes to them.

"We know," Greg blurted out. "The pictures it took. They — "

Spidey's eyes grew wide, his expression angry. "You took pictures with it?"

"Just a few," Greg told him, wishing he had kept his mouth shut. "They didn't come out. Really."

"You know about the camera, then," Spidey said, moving quickly to the center of the floor.

Was he trying to block their escape? Greg wondered.

"It's broken or something," Greg said uncertainly, shoving his hands into his jeans pockets.

"It's not broken," the tall, dark figure said softly. "It's evil." He motioned toward the low plywood table. "Sit there."

Shari and Greg exchanged glances. Then, reluctantly, they sat down on the edge of the board, sitting stiffly, nervously, their eyes darting towards the stairway, towards escape.

"The camera is evil," Spidey repeated, standing over them, holding the camera in both hands. "I should know. I helped to create it."

"You're an inventor?" Greg asked, glancing at Shari, who was nervously tugging at a strand of her black hair.

"I'm a scientist," Spidey replied. "Or, I should say, I *was* a scientist. My name is Fredericks. Dr. Fritz Fredericks." He transferred the camera from one hand to the other. "My lab partner invented this camera. It was his pride and joy. More than that, it would have made him a fortune. *Would* have, I say." He paused, a thoughtful expression sinking over his face.

"What happened to him? Did he die?" Shari asked, still fiddling with the strand of hair.

Dr. Fredericks snickered. "No. Worse. I stole the invention from him. I stole the plans and the camera. I was evil, you see. I was young and greedy. So very greedy. And I wasn't above stealing to make my fortune."

He paused, eyeing them both as if waiting for them to say something, to offer their disapproval of him, perhaps. But when Greg and Shari remained silent, staring up at him from the low plywood table, he continued his story.

"When I stole the camera, it caught my partner by surprise. Unfortunately, from then on, all of the surprises were mine." A strange, sad smile twisted across his aged face. "My partner, you see, was much more evil than I was."

Dr. Fredericks coughed into his hand, then began to pace in front of Greg and Shari as he talked, speaking softly, slowly, as if remembering the story for the first time in a long while.

"My partner was a *true* evil one. He dabbled in

the dark arts. I should correct myself. He didn't just dabble. He was quite a master of it all."

He held up the camera, waving it above his head, then lowering it. "My partner put a curse on the camera. If he couldn't profit from it, he wanted to make sure that I never would, either. And so he put a curse on it."

He turned his gaze on Greg, leaning over him. "Do you know about how some primitive peoples fear the camera? They fear the camera because they believe that if it takes their picture, it will steal their soul." He patted the camera. "Well, this camera really *does* steal souls."

Staring up at the camera, Greg shuddered.

The camera had stolen Shari away.

Would it have stolen *all* of their souls?

"People have died because of this camera," Dr. Fredericks said, uttering a slow, sad sigh. "People close to me. That is how I came to learn of the curse, to learn of the camera's evil. And then I learned something just as frightening — the camera cannot be destroyed."

He coughed, cleared his throat noisily, and began to pace in front of them again. "And so I vowed to keep the camera a secret. To keep it away from people so it cannot do its evil. I lost my job. My family. I lost everything because of it. But I am determined to keep the camera where it can do no harm."

He stopped pacing with his back towards them.

123

He stood silently, shoulders hunched, lost in thought.

Greg quickly climbed to his feet and motioned for Shari to do the same. "Well . . . uh . . . I guess it's good we returned it," he said hesitantly. "Sorry we caused so much trouble."

"Yeah, we're very sorry," Shari repeated sincerely. "Guess it's back in the right hands."

"Good-bye," Greg said, starting towards the steps. "It's getting late, and we — "

"No!" Dr. Fredericks shouted, startling them both. He moved quickly to block the way. "I'm afraid you can't go. You know too much."

30

"I can never let you leave," Dr. Fredericks said, his face flickering in the blue glow of a lightning flash. He crossed his bony arms in front of his black sweatshirt.

"But we won't tell anyone," Greg said, his voice rising until the words became a plea. "Really."

"Your secret is good with us," Shari insisted, her frightened eyes on Greg.

Dr. Fredericks stared at them menacingly, but didn't reply.

"You can trust us," Greg said, his voice quivering. He cast a frightened glance at Shari.

"Besides," Shari said, "even if we *did* tell anyone, who would believe us?"

"Enough talk," Dr. Fredericks snapped. "It won't do you any good. I've worked too long and too hard to keep the camera a secret."

A rush of wind pushed against the windows, sending up a low howl. The wind carried a drumroll of rain. The sky through the basement windows was as black as night.

"You — can't keep us here *forever*!" Shari cried, unable to keep the growing terror from her voice.

The rain pounded against the windows now, a steady downpour.

Dr. Fredericks drew himself up straight, seemed to grow taller. His tiny eyes burned into Shari's. "I'm so sorry," he said, his voice a whisper of regret. "So sorry. But I have no choice."

He took another step towards them.

Greg and Shari exchanged frightened glances. From where they stood, in front of the low plywood table in the center of the basement, the steps seemed a hundred miles away.

"Wh-what are you going to do?" Greg cried, shouting over a burst of thunder that rattled the basement windows.

"Please — !" Shari begged. "Don't — !"

Dr. Fredericks moved forward with surprising speed. Holding the camera in one hand, he grabbed Greg's shoulder with the other.

"No!" Greg screamed. "Let go!"

"Let go of him!" Shari screamed.

She suddenly realized that both of Dr. Frederick's hands were occupied.

This may be my only chance, she thought.

She took a deep breath and lunged forward.

Dr. Fredericks' eyes bulged, and he cried out

in surprise as Shari grabbed the camera with both hands and pulled it away from him. He made a frantic grab for the camera, and Greg burst free.

Before the desperate man could take another step, Shari raised the camera to her eye and pointed the lens at him.

"Please — no! Don't push the button!" the old man cried.

He lurched forward, his eyes wild, and grabbed the camera with both hands.

Greg stared in horror as Shari and Dr. Fredericks grappled, both holding onto the camera, each trying desperately to wrestle it away from the other.

FLASH!

The bright burst of light startled them all.

Shari grabbed the camera. "Run!" she screamed.

31

The basement became a whirring blur of grays and blacks as Greg hurtled himself towards the stairs.

He and Shari ran side by side, slipping over the food cartons, jumping over tin cans and empty bottles.

Rain thundered against the windows. The wind howled, pushing against the glass. They could hear Dr. Fredericks' anguished screams behind them.

"Did it take our picture or his?" Shari asked.

"I don't know. Just *hurry*!" Greg screamed.

The old man was howling like a wounded animal, his cries competing with the rain and wind pushing at the windows.

The stairs weren't that far away. But it seemed to take forever to reach them.

Forever.

Forever, Greg thought. Dr. Fredericks wanted to keep Shari and him down there *forever*.

Panting loudly, they both reached the dark stairway. A deafening clap of thunder made them stop and turn around.

"Huh?" Greg cried aloud.

To his shock, Dr. Fredericks hadn't chased after them.

And his anguished cries had stopped.

The basement was silent.

"What's going on?" Shari cried breathlessly.

Squinting back into the darkness, it took Greg a while to realize that the dark, rumpled form lying on the floor in front of the worktable was Dr. Fredericks.

"What happened?" Shari cried, her chest heaving as she struggled to catch her breath. Still clinging to the camera strap, she gaped in surprise at the old man's still body, sprawled on its back on the floor.

"I don't know," Greg replied in a breathless whisper.

Reluctantly, Greg started back towards Dr. Fredericks. Following close behind, Shari uttered a low cry of horror when she clearly saw the fallen man's face.

Eyes bulged out, the mouth open in a twisted O of terror, the face stared up at them. Frozen. Dead.

Dr. Fredericks was dead.

"What — *happened*?" Shari finally managed to say, swallowing hard, forcing herself to turn away from the ghastly, tortured face.

"I think he died of fright," Greg replied, squeezing her shoulder and not even realizing it.

"Huh? Fright?"

"He knew better than anyone what the camera could do," Greg said. "When you snapped his picture, I think . . . I think it scared him to *death*!"

"I only wanted to throw him off-guard," Shari cried. "I only wanted to give us a chance to escape. I didn't think — "

"The picture," Greg interrupted. "Let's see the picture."

Shari raised the camera. The photo was still half-inside the camera. Greg pulled it out with a trembling hand. He held it up so they could both see it.

"Wow," he exclaimed quietly. "Wow."

The photo showed Dr. Fredericks lying on the floor, his eyes bulging, his mouth frozen open in horror.

Dr. Fredericks' fright, Greg realized — the fright that had killed him — was there, frozen on film, frozen on his face.

The camera had claimed another victim. This time, forever.

"What do we do now?" Shari asked, staring down at the figure sprawled at their feet.

"First, I'm putting this camera back," Greg said, taking it from her and shoving it back on its shelf. He turned the vise handle, and the door to the secret compartment closed.

Greg breathed a sigh of relief. Hiding the dreadful camera away made him feel so much better.

"Now, let's go home and call the police," he said.

Two days later, a cool, bright day with a gentle breeze rustling the trees, the four friends stopped at the curb, leaning on their bikes, and stared up at the Coffman house. Even in bright sunlight, the old trees that surrounded the house covered it in shade.

"So you didn't tell the police about the camera?" Bird asked, staring up at the dark, empty front window.

"No. They wouldn't believe it," Greg told him. "Besides, the camera should stay locked up forever. *Forever!* I hope no one ever finds out about it."

"We told the police we ran into the house to get out of the rain," Shari added. "And we said we started to explore while we waited for the storm to blow over. And we found the body in the basement."

"What did Spidey die of?" Michael asked, gazing up at the house.

"The police said it was heart failure," Greg told him. "But we know the truth."

"Wow. I can't believe one old camera could do so much evil," Bird said.

"I believe it," Greg said quietly.

"Let's get out of here," Michael urged. He raised his sneakers to the pedals and started to roll away. "This place really creeps me out."

The other three followed, pedaling away in thoughtful silence.

They had turned the corner and were heading up the next block when two figures emerged from the back door of the Coffman house. Joey Ferris and Mickey Ward stepped over the weed-choked lawn onto the driveway.

"Those jerks aren't too bright," Joey told his companion. "They never even saw us the other day. Never saw us watching them through the basement window."

Mickey laughed. "Yeah. They're jerks."

"They couldn't hide this camera from *us*. No way, man," Joey said. He raised the camera and examined it.

"Take my picture," Mickey demanded. "Come on. Let's try it out."

"Yeah. Okay." Joey raised the viewfinder to his eye. "Say cheese."

A click. A flash. A whirring sound.

Joey pulled the snapshot from the camera, and both boys eagerly huddled around it, waiting to see what developed.

Add *more*

to your collection . . .

Here's a chilling preview of

THE CURSE OF THE MUMMY'S TOMB

1

There was a loud knock on the door. The bellhop, a bent-over old man who didn't look as if he could pick up a feather pillow, had arrived to take the bags.

Mom and Dad, looking very worried, gave me hugs and more final instructions, and told me once again to stay in the room. The door closed behind them, and it was suddenly very quiet.

Very quiet.

I turned up the TV just to make it a little noisier. The game show had gone off, and now a man in a white suit was reading the news in Arabic.

"I'm not scared," I said aloud. But I had kind of a tight feeling in my throat.

I walked to the window and looked out. The sun was nearly down. The shadow of the skyscraper slanted over the street and onto the hotel.

I picked up my Coke glass and took a sip. It was watery and flat. My stomach growled. I suddenly realized that I was hungry.

Room service, I thought.

Then I decided I'd better not. What if I called and they only spoke Arabic?

I glanced at the clock. Seven-twenty. I wished Uncle Ben would arrive.

I wasn't scared. I just wished he'd arrive.

Okay. Maybe I was a little nervous.

I paced back and forth for a bit. I tried playing *Tetris* on the Game Boy, but I couldn't concentrate, and the light wasn't very good.

Sari is probably a champ at *Tetris*, I thought bitterly.

Where *were* they? What was taking so long?

I began to have horrible, frightening thoughts: What if they can't find the hotel? What if they get mixed up and go to the wrong hotel?

What if they're in a terrible car crash and die? And I'm all by myself in Cairo for days and days?

I know. They were dumb thoughts. But they're the kind of thoughts you have when you're alone in a strange place, waiting for someone to come.

I glanced down and realized I had taken the mummy hand out of my jeans pocket.

It was small, the size of a child's hand. A little hand wrapped in papery brown gauze. I had bought it at a garage sale a few years ago, and I always carried it around as a good luck charm.

The kid who sold it to me called it a "Summoner." He said it was used to summon evil spirits, or something. I didn't care about that. I just thought it was an outstanding bargain for two dollars. I mean, what a great thing to find at a garage sale! And maybe it was even real.

I tossed it from hand to hand as I paced the length of the living room. The TV was starting to make me nervous, so I clicked it off.

But now the quiet was making me nervous.

I slapped the mummy hand against my palm and kept pacing.

Where were they? They should've been here by now.

I was beginning to think that I'd made the wrong choice. Maybe I should've gone to Alexandria with Mom and Dad.

Then I heard a noise at the door. Footsteps.

Was it them?

I stopped in the middle of the living room and listened, staring past the narrow front hallway to the door.

The light was dim in the hallway, but I saw the doorknob turn.

That's strange, I thought. Uncle Ben would knock first — wouldn't he?

The doorknob turned. The door started to creak open.

"Hey — " I called out, but the word choked in my throat.

Uncle Ben would knock. He wouldn't just barge in.

Slowly, slowly, the door squeaked open as I

stared, frozen in the middle of the room, unable to call out.

Standing in the doorway stood a tall, shadowy figure.

I gasped as the figure lurched into the room, and I saw it clearly. Even in the dim light, I could see what it was.

A mummy.

Glaring at me with round, dark eyes through holes in its ancient, thick bandages.

A mummy.

Pushing itself off the wall and staggering stiffly toward me into the living room, its arms outstretched as if to grab me.

I opened my mouth to scream, but no sound came out.

About the Author

R.L. STINE is the author of the series *Fear Street*, *Nightmare Room*, *Give Yourself Goosebumps*, and the phenomenally successful *Goosebumps*. His thrilling teen titles have sold more than 250 million copies internationally — enough to earn him a spot in the *Guinness Book of World Records*! Mr. Stine lives in New York City with his wife, Jane, and his son, Matt.

YOU'VE READ THE BOOKS...
NOW OWN THE THRILLS ON DVD

BRING HOME THE EXCITEMENT!

**R.L. Stine Classics
Come To DVD
For The First Time
From Twentieth Century
Fox Home Entertainment!**

www.foxhome.com

SCHOLASTIC

www.scholastic.com/